Praise for the Red Carpet Catering Mystery Series

MURDER ON A SILVER PLATTER (#1)

"Delicious! A great read written by someone who knows the behind the scenes world of filmmaking...a winner!"

– Kathryn Leigh Scott,
Author of the Jinx Fogarty Mysteries

"Loved this book! The characters are well-drawn and it's cleverly plotted. Totally engrossing...I felt as though I was actually on a movie set. The author is well-versed in her setting and she is able to keep the reader in suspense. I can't wait for the second book in the series."

– Marianna Heusler,
Edgar-Nominated Author

MURDER ON THE HALF SHELL (#2)

"This nicely woven drama once again gave us an insight into catering (what a hard job) while keeping me intrigued in a mystery with some twisty currents that was hard to put down. With a nice island flavor, a nice puzzling mystery and a great cast of characters, this was a very enjoyable read."

– *Dru's Book Musings*

"The writing is fun, quirky and engaging. The character development between the lead character and her love interest is well done and believable. This book has several of my favorite things at the forefront: movies, murder, and food prep."

– *Goodreads*

MURDER
ON THE
HALF SHELL

The Red Carpet Catering Mystery Series
by Shawn Reilly Simmons

MURDER ON A SILVER PLATTER (#1)
MURDER ON THE HALF SHELL (#2)
MURDER ON A DESIGNER DIET (#3)

MURDER
ON THE
HALF SHELL

A RED CARPET CATERING MYSTERY

SHAWN REILLY
SIMMONS

HENERY PRESS

MURDER ON THE HALF SHELL
A Red Carpet Catering Mystery
Part of the Henery Press Mystery Collection

Second Edition
Trade paperback edition | February 2016

Henery Press, LLC
www.henerypress.com

ISBN-13: 978-1-943390-61-8

Printed in the United States of America

For My Mom

ACKNOWLEDGMENTS

Thanks to everyone who supported me during the writing of this book, especially readers whose feedback and excitement has pushed me forward on this journey. It really is a dream come true, which wouldn't be possible without all of you.

I have to thank my mom for moving us to South Florida from Indiana when we were just babies. That showed us that big moves are possible, and a lot of times things turn out for the better if you just take a chance.

Thanks to the entire mystery writing community, and everyone at Malice Domestic for all the love and encouragement. Knowing you all have my back makes it easier to stay in the writing chair.

Thanks to Ildy Shannon for being my first reader, and for all the valuable input and suggestions.

Heartfelt thanks go out to Kendel Lynn and Art Molinares at Henery Press. None of this would be possible without you, and I'm so happy to be a part of your team. I can't say enough about the positive guidance from Rachel Jackson and Erin George: your work on the books is invaluable and I'm forever grateful.

As always, without the love and support from Matthew and Russell, I wouldn't be able to do all the things I do. Their love and patience push me through.

CHAPTER 1

Arlena Madison sprinted down the beach towards the sea, strands of her long black hair pulling away from the intricate set of pins holding it in a twist at the nape of her neck. When she came to the edge of the water, she stopped and glanced fearfully over her shoulder. Her chest heaved, pressing against the ribs of her corset. She shielded her eyes from the sun and caught a glimpse of the man at the top of the dune. She began to run again, parallel to the shore, the skirt of her long purple dress and petticoat soaking up the warm salt water. The wet sand sucked at her bare feet and her dress pulled at her shoulders, her steps becoming more difficult with each step. Foamy waves slapped her calves as she struggled to stay upright.

"Jane, stop this instant!" the man yelled from behind her as he slid down the dunes in his shiny black dress shoes, the tails of his morning coat flapping behind him.

At the sound of his voice, Arlena paused. She gazed out at the sea, refusing to turn and look at him. Sweat beaded her temples and dampened the hair now clumped around her shoulders.

"Darling, what has gotten into you?" he pleaded as he ran towards her.

She closed her eyes. After a moment of hesitation, she set

her shoulders and began walking into the water.

"Jane, don't," the man called out with exasperation. He tripped in the sand and fell to his knees, reaching out for Arlena, who moved determinedly into the water.

Arlena gazed out at the horizon, squinting against the bright sun as the waves lapped against her, darkening the fabric of her dress up to her waist.

The man pulled himself to his feet, awkwardly running the rest of the way to the water. "Jane, Thomas and I need you."

Arlena's shoulders caved. She placed a hand over her mouth and turned to him. "John, please help me." She struggled to turn back towards the shore.

He quickly pulled off his jacket and shoes and waded into the ocean as Arlena struggled towards him, gathering up her heavy skirts beneath the water. He hooked an arm around her waist as a tall wave crashed over them.

Sweeping up Arlena's slender frame, he made his way back to shore, the waves ushering him along from behind. Collapsing onto the dry sand, he crushed Arlena to his chest and brushed a few strands of hair from her face. "What demons have possessed you, my blessed little goose?" He kissed her quickly on the lips then gazed out at the ocean as he rocked her.

"Cut!" a man's voice shouted loudly behind them. The camera loader slapped the digital clapperboard that read "*The Yellow Wallpaper*, Beach Scene 4: Take 8" in front of the nearest camera lens.

Arlena's eyes popped open. "Nice ad lib with the kiss."

"You liked that one, huh, love?" Gavin McKenna said, smiling down at her. He held her in his arms a beat longer, then helped her into a seated position next to him.

Arlena sighed and settled onto the warm sand. Untangling the heavy skirts from her legs she said, "Sure. We'll see what

Shane thinks of it."

"Speak of the devil," Gavin said as the director approached them. He straightened his legs and attempted to brush the wet sand from his wool dress pants without success.

Shane crouched down next to his stars, his carrot-colored hair barely contained by his baseball cap. "Nicely done, you two. Let's reset and do it again from one."

Shane jumped up without another word and shouted at the cameraman standing at the edge of the water in yellow wading pants. The camera on his shoulder had been draped with a clear plastic bag to protect it from the waves.

"Again?" Gavin said after Shane was out of earshot. "Maybe he'd like to tell us what he wants us to do differently, eh?"

Penelope Sutherland, head chef on the movie set, stepped outside the catering tent and saw Arlena and Gavin chatting together on the sand. She'd watched them roll through the last take, the eighth one for this scene. They'd been filming variations of it all morning, spending hours going from dry to wet and back to dry to capture what would amount to a few minutes of screen time. Penelope and her team were ready to serve lunch after prepping and cooking for six hours, ever since they'd served and cleaned up after breakfast.

"We're going again," a faint voice sputtered from the walkie-talkie Penelope had clipped on the front pocket of her apron. "Everyone back to one."

Penelope, hands on her hips, raised her palm to her sweaty forehead and turned around. The tent was filled with salads, desserts, roasted fish and chicken, vegetables and hot and cold sides. Her four chefs had all changed into fresh white jackets, *Red Carpet Catering* stitched in bold red letters on their chests, after sweating through the ones they'd worn during prep. They were lined up in a row, ready to serve the one hundred and thirty-seven people scheduled to eat that day.

She unclipped the walkie-talkie from her apron pocket and pressed the button.

"Catering to production," she said into the little black box.

"Go catering," a thin voice scratched back at her.

"Lunch is ready, at the time requested. Are we breaking?" A bead of sweat slid down her spine underneath her chef's coat.

"Nope, doing another take. Shane says to put everything on ice," the voice came back.

Penelope squeezed the walkie-talkie tightly in her hand and blew out a loud sigh. Pressing the button again she said, "What's the ETA on breaking?"

"Maybe twenty. We'll let you know." The voice snapped off with a loud chirp. Penelope squinted into the sun and tried to see who she had been talking to on the other end. She couldn't tell which assistant director or production assistant was speaking on behalf of the director. It definitely wasn't Shane. His high-pitched voice was very distinctive.

Penelope turned around and stepped back into the large white tent. "They're going to be late," she said, attempting to hide the frustration in her voice.

"Again? The ice is melting already, Boss," Francis said, nodding his head in the direction of the salad bar. Frosted bowls filled with cut fruit, vegetables and a variety of cold salads perched on top of chipped ice inside large tubs lined the edge of the tent. The ice would keep the food fresh and safe to eat during service, as long as it stayed frozen, but she could see the ice was already glassy looking. It didn't stand much of a chance against the heat.

Penelope eyed their setup, proud of how perfect everything

looked before the crew would come through scooping and grabbing at the food. "Let's wait five minutes, drain off the water and fill the bins back up with ice. Try to keep things looking good until they get here."

Quentin slapped a white service towel over his shoulder. "Why do they bother giving us a break time if they never come close to it?"

Francis chuckled. "There's worse things in life. We're in paradise, right?"

Quentin sucked his teeth. "Whatever. I didn't know paradise would be so humid." The other chefs murmured in agreement behind him, all of them hot and cranky.

"We do the best we can," Penelope broke in, attempting to get her team to refocus. "If something looks like it's dying, just pull it off and walk it back up to the refrigerator on the truck. Where are the girls?"

"Break area, I think," Francis said.

A few minutes later, Penelope walked around to the rear of the tent to look for her servers, a couple of high school students she had hired to waitress part time on the set. They were in the designated break area, a half circle of folding chairs and a large piece of driftwood they had fashioned into a table. It was partially shaded by the eave of the tent. The girls sat with their heads touching, a single set of earbuds shared between them, staring at the phone in Rebekkah's palm. Rebekkah rubbed Sabena's back lightly, drawing lazy circles in the center. They didn't notice Penelope approaching until her shadow fell across their legs.

Rebekkah looked up first, clicking her phone off quickly and placing it upside down in her lap. "Miss Sutherland, are you ready for us to come in?" she asked, pulling the bud from her ear.

"No, they're running late. Again. What are you two up to?"

Sabena blinked behind her pink plastic sunglasses, leaving her earbud in place. Her expression was flat, either grim or bored, Penelope couldn't tell. Rebekkah pulled her hand slowly from Sabena's back and placed it limply in her lap, palm up, glittery pink nail polish chipping her fingernails.

Rebekkah cut her eyes at her friend. "Nothing. Listening to music." Sabena turned to watch a wave roll onto the sand. The girls sat with their legs crossed towards each other, perching on the edge of the hot metal chairs, not seeming to mind the sun baking their thighs.

"No phones inside during service," Penelope said. "We're getting started in twenty, hopefully."

The girls gazed at her silently.

"Have you seen Regan?" Penelope asked, glancing up the beach where her catering trucks were parked.

They shook their heads in unison. Penelope turned to go, taking a look back at them after a few steps. Rebekkah had replaced her earbud, and they were focused on the phone again.

Penelope walked up the dunes to check on her newly hired helper. She blinked several times after entering the kitchen truck, willing her eyes to adjust to the dark interior. Regan was in the front corner, scrubbing a sheet pan in a sink filled with sudsy water. The kitchen was clean, the counters had been wiped down and a stack of dishes was drying on the counter. Regan looked over his shoulder at her, breaking into a grin as she approached.

"Kitchen looks good," Penelope said. "When you're finished, come to the tent. We may have to run food back and forth."

"Sure, Boss," Regan said, turning off the water and drying his hands.

"Would you like to stay on with us through the rest of the shoot?" Penelope asked, leaning her waist against the counter and crossing her arms. "You're a good worker, and we can use the help."

"I'd love to," Regan said. "I can cook on the line too, if you need extra hands in the kitchen."

"Let me know your availability and I'll put you on the schedule," Penelope said, turning to leave.

Back on the beach, Penelope watched Gavin McKenna undressing Arlena on the sand as various members of the crew rushed around them, resetting the beach scene.

"Someone radio wardrobe to come and help me with this," Arlena called to a passing PA, her dark red curls tangled in earphones. The girl stopped short and looked at Arlena's wet dress lying in the sand. She said something into her headset and hurried away.

Gavin patted Arlena's shoulder from behind. "Your corset as well, my lady?" he asked, glancing at the cinched top piece and white underskirt that was soaked midway up Arlena's chest. An unlit cigarette bounced from the corner of his mouth as he spoke.

"Please. Get this thing off of me," Arlena said gratefully.

Gavin unlaced her bodice and it fell to the sand, revealing Arlena's flesh-colored Spanx body suit. Wardrobe had given her one made from moisture-wicking material, so she was relatively dry under her wet costume.

Gavin glanced down at his leading lady's tightly fitting undergarment. "You look much more comfortable now."

Arlena punched him playfully on the arm. "I know. Everyone is so worried about how comfortable we are. You're lucky Spanx for Men isn't a thing."

"It's a cruel world, isn't it?" Gavin teased as he lit his cigarette.

"You know those things will kill you, right?" Arlena asked, stepping away from the smoke.

Gavin winked at her. "Not right away. Besides, I have to smoke these or I'll end up needing Spanx for Men." He glanced behind him towards the catering tent farther up the beach. "I thought we'd be eating by now. Weren't we supposed to break for lunch already?"

Arlena shook her head and shrugged. She shielded her eyes, sweeping them towards the catering tent and catching a glimpse of Penelope ducking back inside.

"Why aren't they in wardrobe?" Shane stormed up from behind them, waving wildly at Arlena and Gavin. Everyone jumped a little, except Gavin, who had the advantage of seeing him coming.

"They're going now," the young PA stammered, her already red face darkening even more. "Right this way, Miss Madison...Mr. McKenna," she said, pointing urgently towards the wardrobe tent at the edge of the dunes.

"Arlena, you're doing great," Shane said in a gentler tone of voice. "Everything is almost perfect. I need the shot again to cut in a different angle, and I need the same light as the last one."

Arlena smiled. "Of course, Shane, whatever you say."

"It's Friday, and I've got a big surprise for everyone tonight," Shane said, ushering Arlena toward the dunes. "We just have to push through and get this shot." The wardrobe and makeup teams would slip Arlena and Gavin into exact copies of their clothes, re-pin Arlena's hair and touch up their makeup in less than ten minutes.

"Gavin, are you coming?" Arlena asked over her shoulder

as she began walking up the beach.

"Right behind you," he said, waving his cigarette.

CHAPTER 2

"You just crack their heads off like this." *Snap!* "And then suck out the juice."

Penelope watched as the man's thick fingers twisted the head off of a crawfish. He raised the little red head to his lips and sucked it clean. Her stomach did a flip when he handed one to her to try.

"That's okay," she said, glancing around to see what else was being served for dinner.

"Come on. Don't tell me a brave girl like you is afraid of little Crusty here. You have to have one," he said, motioning for her to take the sea creature from his grubby hand.

Penelope accepted it, pinching it between two fingers.

"Here, give me that." He gestured toward her clear plastic cup filled halfway with white wine.

Penelope reluctantly handed it over, watching it disappear behind his thick knuckles. Earlier that afternoon, as Penelope and her crew finally served lunch after a forty-minute delay, Shane had announced he'd arranged a beach party for the entire cast and crew to celebrate the end of the long filming week. She'd been looking forward to it ever since.

By the time the cast and crew finally broke for lunch, her staff had to pull the tray of salmon off the line because it had gotten too dry, but they were able to salvage most everything else. Penelope had to admit she'd been thinking about a crisp glass or two of Sauvignon Blanc all day. She hadn't particularly been looking forward to pulling apart a boiled crawfish for dinner. Somehow it felt like she was back at work in the kitchen.

"You'll thank me after you taste it."

Penelope leaned forward slightly, holding the crawfish away from her body with a crooked arm, afraid she would dribble its juice on her short white sundress. She looked into the eyes of the crawfish and then into the eyes of Emilio Babineau, celebrity chef and owner of Craw Daddy's, a popular restaurant in New Orleans, and coincidentally her former culinary school instructor. She pinched the head between two fingers and began to twist, separating it from the body.

"There you go," Emilio said, chuckling. "Now, suck it out."

"Really?" Penelope asked. "I use shrimp heads for making seafood stock, but I've never been tempted to suck on one."

"It's a delicacy. You won't believe the flavor in there."

Penelope scrunched up her nose and placed the crawfish head between her lips, trying to shake the image of tiny crawfish brains. When she pulled the liquid into her mouth, all doubt fell away as she tasted the spicy brine. "Oh man, that is good." She wiped her chin with the back of her hand, the crawfish's head still pinched between her fingers.

"Just like a baby lobster," Emilio said.

The table next to them was piled high with boiled crawfish, shrimp, corn and potatoes, all resting on a layer of newspaper. A few members of the film crew stood nearby, drinking beers and picking through the food. Penelope slid her feet out of her sandals and spread her toes in the sand, which was still warm even though the sun was setting over the ocean. She shifted her weight back and forth, giving her tired feet a mini massage.

Arlena approached them, her black sundress rippling in the wind, revealing evenly tanned legs. She glanced at the table piled high with crawfish, and Penelope saw the briefest moment of disgust slip across her face.

"Emilio, this is Arlena Madison," Penelope said, introducing them. "Emilio was one of my chef instructors at culinary school. Shane flew him down from New Orleans to throw this party for us tonight."

Emilio gazed at Arlena. "I've seen all your movies. You're even more beautiful in person."

"Thank you," Arlena said, smiling graciously. She then turned to Penelope and said, "Sam's not coming this weekend, but he sent the boat. Since we're off for a few days, I was thinking we could stay on it together. Take a break?"

"Sam Cavanaugh?" Emilio asked. "So the tabloids are right. You two are an item?" He flipped open the cooler that was wedged in the sand nearby, plunging his hand into the ice water and grabbing a beer. He seemed to remember just then that he was holding Penelope's plastic cup of wine and handed it back to her. She took it from him, disappointed that it was now warm to the touch and smudged with crawfish juice.

"Sure," Penelope said to Arlena. "It will be nice to get away."

"Hey, you want a crawfish?" Emilio asked. He turned and scooped a handful of them from the table, shaking off the excess liquid onto the sand, and took a step towards Arlena.

Although he was still well away from her, Arlena took an awkward step backwards. Her foot caught in her long dress and she lost her balance. Penelope grabbed her forearm, stopping her from falling over.

"Damn, girl, you okay? These critters are long gone, ain't gonna bite ya."

His New Orleans drawl was becoming more pronounced with each beer.

"Arlena's allergic to shellfish, Chef," Penelope said.

"Really? Now that's a damn shame. Not even a tiny little crawfish?"

"Nope," Arlena said, giving him a tight smile.

"And here I am, the Crawfish King of Louisiana. Looks like things won't work out between us after all." Emilio laughed loudly at his own joke.

Penelope motioned with her glass to the thatch-roofed bar perched on the beach behind them. "Drink?"

"Absolutely," Arlena said, flicking her eyes at Emilio. He beamed at her, an icy beer in one hand and crawfish dangling from the other.

"Excuse us, Chef," Penelope said, picking up her sandals and leading Arlena up the beach towards the bar.

The sun was just setting for the day and a loose circle of tiki torches flickered in the breeze, marking off the space for the party. Penelope was relieved she and her crew had the night off and that someone else had to do all of the cooking and cleanup for a change.

Penelope ordered two glasses of wine and asked the bartender for some wet wipes. She tore open the foil packs and wiped the spot on Arlena's arm where she had touched her, and then carefully wiped away the crawfish residue from her hands and underneath her fingernails.

"That guy was your teacher?" Arlena asked a bit incredulously.

"Yes, he taught fish kitchen. Actually, he gave me a letter of recommendation that helped me get my first job after school." Penelope glanced over her shoulder at the growing crowd on the beach, noticing her crew grouped together at one of the tables.

Gavin ducked around a few partygoers and approached the bar. "Hello, ladies. Penelope, it's nice to see you out of your apron."

"Are you recovered from this long week of work?" Penelope asked.

"Not quite." He pulled a thin silver flask from the pocket of his pants and took a swig. Penelope could smell the distinct tang of whiskey. "But I will be soon." He offered the flask to Penelope who waved it away. He pulled his cigarettes from his other pocket, an odd-sized pack with an unfamiliar holographic design on the front.

"What are those?" Penelope asked.

"Lambert & Butlers," Gavin replied, eyeing the pack before slipping it into his shirt pocket. "I had to pay duty on the extra cartons I brought over with me. Luckily more will be coming my way next week."

"They don't sell something you can smoke at Rose's?" Arlena asked, crinkling her nose.

"I'm hopelessly British, I'm afraid," Gavin said. "I can't smoke tobacco from Virginia, USA, wherever that is. I sound like a snob, don't I?"

"It just adds to your charm," Arlena said. "America is going to embrace you when this movie comes out. Then maybe you'll appreciate our cigarettes."

"From your lips," Gavin said.

"Penelope, over here!"

Penelope followed the shout and saw Emilio, who had been joined by Shane, waving her over. Penelope sighed and rolled her eyes at Arlena. "Be right back."

"Duty calls," Gavin said.

Penelope made her way down the beach, feeling the warm breeze blow through her thin dress.

"Emilio says you were his student," Shane said.

"That's right, several years ago," Penelope said, nodding, "About seven now. I was sorry when you left—"

"To open the restaurant," Emilio said quickly, clapping Shane on the back. "When those kinds of opportunities arise you have to go for it."

Shane choked on a mouthful of beer. After recovering he said, "Small world, huh?"

"It sure is," Emilio agreed.

"How do you guys know each other?" Penelope asked.

"I've been a fan of Craw Daddy's for a while now," Shane said. "I eat there every time I'm in New Orleans. Me and Emilio got to know each other, and now I'm an investor in the restaurants."

"Restaurants?" Penelope asked. "I didn't know you had more than one."

A gust of wind blew the tails of Emilio's Hawaiian shirt up, and Penelope caught a glimpse of his belly. He wasn't overweight, but he'd definitely gotten softer around the middle since school. He also seemed to have more tattoos than she remembered, having seen him sunbathing behind the kitchen classroom on more than one occasion. He now had a cartoon drawing of a smiling crawfish on his left calf and his restaurant's logo blazed across the right. His arms were covered in flames, licking upwards as if they had caught fire on a hot grill.

"Craw Daddy's is expanding," Shane said, slapping Emilio's bicep.

"We're opening up our new location right here." Emilio swept his arm in an arc, motioning at the white sand and ocean, rocking forward as he gestured. Penelope glanced at the cooler next to Emilio's feet and wondered how many beers were left inside.

"You're opening a restaurant on this little island?" Penelope asked.

"Yeah, and I'm remodeling an old house for a vacation home here too. This guy is a great salesman." Emilio swung and almost missed Shane's bicep in a return punch. "I've got the original place in New Orleans and one opening in Atlanta, and we're looking at Miami," Emilio said with an amazed expression.

"Wow, that's a lot of ground to cover," Penelope said. "How did all of this happen?"

"Shane here has the Andrea Island connections, but he wants to take Craw Daddy's to the next level. He introduced me to the powers that be up in town and they dig it. Well, most of them," Emilio mumbled, shrugging again and taking another swig from his bottle. "Shane thinks it will be a big draw for people to come here, you know, the exclusive VIP celebrity crowd. 'Dine in paradise at the Andrea Island Craw Daddy's.' That kind of thing." Emilio motioned with his hands as if reading off of a marquee in the sky, his beer bottle dangling between his thumb and forefinger.

"I know it will be my favorite place to eat. And I'll bring lots of friends," Shane said, nodding.

"Well, congratulations, Chef," Penelope said. "I'm really happy for you."

Emilio paused, as if he was trying to remember something. After a few seconds, he appeared to abandon the thought and said, "Shane has some great contacts here. Found the restaurant location for me, everything, really. Everyone likes seafood, right?" He laughed again, his cheeks bright red under his dark five o'clock shadow. His spiky black hair was holding up surprisingly well in the Florida humidity. "Well, not everybody," he murmured, raising his beer bottle in a toast towards the bar behind them and taking a long look at Arlena.

"I remember coming here with my sister when we were younger," Shane said to no one in particular. "Our parents would load us up first thing in the morning and drive half the day, cross over the ferry to get here. This was our favorite place to visit when we were kids." His eyes lost focus for a moment.

Emilio and Shane began reminiscing about a restaurant they frequented in Vegas. Penelope excused herself when they moved on to musing over some aspiring actress they had met there who offered to do an audition for Shane during dinner. Penelope was relieved to have missed the end of that story, embarrassed for the woman they were discussing in less than flattering terms.

Penelope walked back toward the bar, taking another look at her team as she passed. Her gaze stopped short and a pin pricked her stomach when she noticed a beer bottle dangling from Regan's hand as he talked to the group. Rebekkah and Sabena gazed at him intently, both of them glassy eyed and hanging on his every word. The girls were dressed alike in tiny white shorts and pink tank tops, long ponytails and matching hoop earrings brushing their shoulders.

"Regan?" Penelope approached her team from behind, interrupting him. "Can I talk to you for a second?"

"Miss Sutherland," Regan said. He didn't attempt to hide the beer from her. "Sure."

Sabena and Rebekkah leaned closer to each other, their water bottles dripping condensation onto the sand. Rebekkah pulled out a bright pink tube of lip gloss from her tiny silver cross-body purse. She swiped her lips with the sparkly liquid, then offered it to Sabena, who to Penelope's surprise, accepted it and swiped her own lips. Penelope didn't like drinking out of someone else's water glass, much less using their freshly swiped lipstick wand. Sabena rubbed her lips together and tucked the tube into her back pocket. The faint smell of artificial strawberries wafted towards Penelope. She refocused on Regan.

"Are you drinking a beer?" Penelope asked. She stood on the dune, the downward slope of the sand giving her more height.

"Yes, do you want one?" Regan asked. He took a step towards the cooler propped in the sand next to the picnic table.

"No. Regan, are you twenty-one?" Penelope asked, crossing her arms over her chest.

Regan's eyes lit up. "Almost...in a year and a half."

"That's what I thought," Penelope said. "I just filled out your paperwork for payroll. You're old enough to work but not old enough to drink." She made eye contact with Francis, who shook his head sheepishly.

"Oh, right. My parents let me drink as long as I'm not driving. I'm sorry, I forgot. It's an island rule."

Penelope looked into his eyes and could see he wasn't lying. "The thing is, it's not really allowed, legally, in the rest of the country. The production could be held liable, and me personally, if anything happened to you."

"Sorry, Boss," Regan said. He drained the bottle onto the sand and tossed it into the trash barrel. "I'll stick to soda from now on."

Penelope turned to the girls. "I know for sure you are both way too young to be drinking."

Rebekkah grinned and showed Penelope her water bottle. "Just water. We signed a pledge at school."

"What kind of pledge?" Penelope asked.

"No drinking, no cheating, no drugs, you know. The usual," Sabena chimed in.

Regan sniffed a quick laugh as he dug around in the cooler for a soda.

Penelope sighed. "I'm not going to make you sign anything like that. I trust your judgment, but don't let me down, or you won't be asked back to the set."

The girls nodded in unison.

"How are you getting home?" Penelope asked.

"Bean's mom is coming to get us," Rebekkah said. "We're sleeping over."

"Okay, have fun tonight. And have a good weekend," Penelope said.

Francis jogged behind Penelope as she walked back up the beach towards the bar. "I should have said something to him about the beer, Boss. I'll make sure he sticks to soda."

"Good. Keep an eye on them too," she said, eyeing Rebekkah and Sabena's tanned legs. Sabena giggled behind her hand at something Regan said and shot a quick glance at Penelope.

Penelope never would've been allowed to drink in high school, or even stay out late at a party. She felt uneasy, the beach suddenly feeling dangerous, the crashing waves reminding her that the ocean swallowed people whole, sweeping them away to where they were never found again. And the thorny brush of the mangrove fields that lined the sand could hide anyone who wanted to stalk a young vulnerable girl at a party.

Penelope willed the paranoid thoughts from her mind and turned away from her team. "Be safe," she said to Francis over her shoulder as she walked away.

CHAPTER 3

Penelope resisted opening her eyelids against the sunlight coming through the little round window of her cabin. She usually had to get up before five in the morning for work, so on her days off she tried to stay in bed as long as possible. When it became clear that she probably wouldn't be able to fall back asleep, she opened her eyes and blinked a few times at the digital clock on the nightstand and saw it was just after seven.

Her phone was charging next to the clock and she unplugged it, glancing at the screen. A sleepy smile came to her lips when she saw a text message from Joey that said, "Good morning, Penny. Miss you. Call you later." Her heart did a little skip as she reread the message.

She typed, "Good morning. Off for the next three days. Staying on Sam's boat. Miss you too."

Penelope had been dating Detective Joseph Baglioni since the previous winter, reconnecting with him during the murder investigation of a young girl who had been found dead outside Penelope's house in New Jersey. Penelope and Joey had gone to school together as kids and had since found they had more in common than just middle school. Things were going well, if a little slowly, but Penelope felt like that might be for the best.

* * *

Penelope borrowed one of the brightly painted bikes the Andrea Island Visitor's Dock made available to guests with a roomy basket in front of the handlebars, which she would need for the groceries she intended to get for the weekend. She and Arlena had left the beach party soon after she had talked to Regan, and spent the night on Sam's yacht, which rocked gently in the last slip of the weathered dock.

Penelope pedaled up the sand-covered asphalt path that led to Ocean Avenue, Andrea Island's main street. When she came to the end of the path, Penelope paused and considered her options. Turning left would take her to Sackler's Market, the only grocery store on the island. She opted to go right, toward Rose's Beach Shop, which sold souvenirs, suntan lotion, sodas and coffee.

The sun wasn't out in full force yet, but the air was already thick with humidity. Sweat pricked Penelope's temples, her pink slip-on Chuck Taylors occasionally sliding off the worn pedals. Ocean Avenue was quiet, the island just beginning to wake up.

Someone had scrawled "Back in Ten" and taped it to the glass on the front door of Rose's. Penelope sighed and stood over her bike, rolling it back and forth between her legs. "Ten what? Minutes? Hours? And when does the ten start?" she muttered. Leaning her bike against a palm tree next to a faded wooden bench on the sidewalk, she peered through the plate-glass window. She could see that the lights were on, but no one was inside. Penelope looked up and down the avenue and then decided to walk around the side of the store to see if Rose's old yellow Volvo was in its usual spot in the gravel parking lot. If it was, she was probably close by, since she lived in the apartment above her shop. Maybe Rose was out back on a smoke break.

As Penelope turned the corner, she tripped over a pair of

outstretched legs. Someone was sitting on the ground, leaning up against the wall, a weathered baseball hat with a blue and white panther on it pulled low on his face to shade the sun.

"Oh geez, I'm sorry," Penelope said, taking a step back and regaining her balance.

The man bent his legs and pulled his knees up to his chest, then peeked out from under the bill of his cap.

"Regan? What are you doing out here?" Penelope asked.

"Nothing."

His head nodded slowly downward, his chin coming to a rest on his chest.

"Regan, are you okay?" Penelope crouched down beside him and shook his shoulder gently. The sour smell of alcohol mixed with the sweat rolled off his skin. "Regan, wake up," Penelope urged.

His eyes fluttered open and he grinned. "Hey, Boss. It's our day off."

"Come on, get up," Penelope said, hooking an arm under his elbow and urging him to stand. Even though he was a lanky kid and Penelope was strong, Regan felt like he was made of cement. After a few attempts, he got his dusty combat boots under his behind in a squatting position, and then pushed himself up to standing, the stucco wall grabbing his t-shirt.

"Come sit over here," Penelope said, pulling him over to the wooden bench on the sidewalk.

"Good morning, Penelope," a raspy voice called from behind her. Rose stood in the doorway of her store, the little note from the window stuck to her finger. Rose pushed the door open and nudged a piece of coral against the base to keep it in place.

"Rose," Penelope said. She glanced back down at Regan, who had nodded off again on the bench.

At least he was up off the ground.

"What's going on over there? You guys okay?" Rose asked, holding her hand up to shield her eyes from the sun.

"I don't know. I think he might be drunk, but I can't imagine how he could be this early in the morning," Penelope said, fists on her hips. Regan slid farther down onto the bench but his eyes stayed closed.

"You never pulled an all-nighter, huh?" Rose chuckled. She pulled a pack of cigarettes out of the pocket of her Capri pants and stepped out onto the sidewalk, shaking one out and clamping it between her frosted lips.

"An all-nighter?" Penelope asked. "I've worked all night many times, but I definitely have never stayed up all night drinking until morning. He's going to feel terrible for days."

"Maybe," Rose said, expelling little streams of smoke out of her nostrils. "But he's a Daniels, so he'll probably be okay."

Penelope shrugged, not exactly sure what she meant. Was Regan Daniels from a family of professional drinkers? Somehow it felt strange to ask Rose to explain, as if she'd be invading Regan's privacy. Penelope glanced up and down the street again. As far as she could tell, they were the only three people awake on the island. Well, two of them were at least.

Rose propped an ankle across the opposite bony knee and rubbed her cigarette in a circular motion on the bottom of her flip flop. The pink rubber sported several burnt spots and Penelope guessed she often used her shoes as makeshift ashtrays. Rose brought her foot down and smeared the smoldering rubbed-off embers into the sandy sidewalk, then returned the half-smoked cigarette to the pack and popped it back into her pocket.

"You want some coffee?" she asked Penelope, brushing some ash off of her pants leg.

"Yes. I'm dying for some," Penelope said. She had started to sweat in earnest from her struggles to get Regan onto the bench. But she still needed a cup of hot coffee before she could think about doing anything else.

"He'll be fine there. Come on in," Rose said, walking back into her store.

Rose's offered an eclectic mix of items ranging from beachwear and souvenirs to quick snacks, cold drinks and cigarettes. Two mismatched metal aisles sat in the middle of the store's wooden floor displaying packs of gum, chips and packaged cupcakes. The aisles were flanked by four spin-racks stuffed with typical beach sundries like sunglasses, plastic keychains, bottle openers and multicolored shot glasses with *Andrea Island* embossed on them. Penelope spun the one closest to the door. It made such a loud screeching sound that she stopped it and quickly stepped away. She made her way to the beverage cooler that sweated in the back corner, its refrigeration unit protesting loudly against the humid air, and grabbed two large bottles of water. Walking along the back wall she looked up at the dusty mural of Andrea Island t-shirts stretched over torso-shaped cardboard cutouts. A woman entered the store and walked quickly to the coolers in the back.

"Here you go," Rose said from behind the wooden counter, placing a large paper cup of coffee next to a plate of homemade brownies wrapped tightly in cellophane. "Anything else for you, Penelope?" Rose's eyes were bright blue beneath her wrinkled eyelids.

"These," Penelope said, grabbing two large oranges out of a weathered crate propped on the floor in front of the counter.

Rose's other customer stood behind her, a large water bottle crooked in her arm. "Excuse me," she said, tapping Penelope's shoulder from behind.

Penelope turned, a bit startled.

"I'm sorry, but are you Penelope from the movie?"

"Yes, Penelope Sutherland."

Penelope searched the woman's face, but wasn't able to place it among the ones she'd met on the island.

"I'm Roni Lambert. Sabena's mom."

"It's nice to meet you," Penelope said. "Sabena's been a big help on the set. Both of the girls have."

Penelope turned back and paid for her items, glancing up at the wooden cabinet nailed to the wall behind the counter. The door had swung open and she could see a few sets of keys dangling from little hooks inside.

"You still have some cabins available?" she asked Rose.

Rose reached up and swung the cabinet door closed, straightening a plastic binder that had *Andrea Island Cabin Rentals* written down the spine. "Just a few, it's been a good summer."

Penelope gathered up her things and stepped away from the counter. "What time did the girls call you to pick them up last night?"

Roni stepped up to the counter, looking a bit confused.

"I didn't pick them up. They were walking home to Rebekkah's after." She dug in her purse for loose change as she spoke.

Penelope's stomach dropped a notch. "Oh, I thought they said they were getting a ride from you."

Roni shrugged and continued to dig in her purse, finally locating a few coins on the bottom. She put them on the counter and pulled out her phone. "No, not last night at least. I do spend a lot of time ferrying them both around. No calls or texts from Bean yet this morning." She studied the phone another few seconds and said, "Which is weird." She flipped open the phone and punched a number. "And right to her voicemail." A look of concern darkened her features as she closed the phone.

"It's early, Roni," Rose said from behind the counter. "What teenager is up at this hour on the weekend?"

"Bean usually is," Roni said, trying the call again. "Call me when you get this," she said sternly to the voicemail. She hung up and punched another number, then hung up without success. "Rebekkah's not answering either."

Penelope took a step away from her and looked at Rose, wishing she hadn't brought anything about the girls up in the first place. "They're probably still asleep, like Rose said. I must have heard them wrong. There was a lot going on."

"Sabena was excited to be invited to the party," Roni said, slipping her phone into her purse and relaxing slightly. "They had our permission to go."

"I'm sure I just got it confused," Penelope said, not sure of that at all, but not wanting to alarm Sabena's mother more than she already had or get the girls into trouble. "Nice meeting you. See you, Rose."

When Penelope walked back outside she saw her bike leaning against the tree next to the park bench, but Regan was gone.

CHAPTER 4

As Penelope pedaled back to the docks she saw a small influx of people emerging from the ferry landing area, a group of older couples in pastel-patterned shorts wearing sun visors, colorful beach totes slung over their shoulders. Penelope eased carefully around the tourists, then returned the loaner bike to the rack at the top of the dock.

The heat of the day was getting into full swing, and Penelope wanted to get the groceries she had picked up at Sackler's in the refrigerator as soon as possible. Her shoulders protested, but she was determined to make it in one trip to the end of the dock where Sam's yacht, the *Isn't She Lovely*, was docked with all of the bags.

She shuffled quickly across the boards, pausing halfway to shift the plastic bags to redistribute the weight. The arm of one of the plastic bags snapped just as she reached the slip and her load was suddenly much lighter on the left side.

"Crap," Penelope said. She looked down and saw a few oranges and grapefruits rolling to the edge of the dock towards the water.

She quickly set the bags down and lunged to the left to grab the renegade citrus, catching one of them quickly. An orange continued to roll and Penelope stumbled towards it, losing her footing and tripping on a raised board on the dock. She skinned her knee and landed in the water into an empty slip across from Sam's boat.

Disoriented and eyes stinging from the salty water, Penelope swam toward the dock, flailing and gasping for air as her head broke the surface.

Suddenly she felt a strong arm reach around her waist and hoist her up. She swiped the saltwater from her eyes and choked on some water when she realized it was Max Madison, Arlena's half-brother.

"Max. What are you doing here?" Penelope sputtered.

"Saving your life, obviously," Max said, managing to look cool and collected as Penelope floundered next to him. He pulled her towards the dock ladder, pushing her gently up and out of the water.

Penelope felt self-conscious as she climbed up the ladder with Max right behind her, realizing he'd have a full view of her wet behind. She hurried up onto the dock, her bare feet slipping on the boards as she looked around for her groceries.

One and then the other of her pink tennis shoes was tossed onto the dock by Max, who held the escaped orange in his hand as he came up out of the water. He was tall and lean with just the right amount of muscle, his wet t-shirt and cargo shorts clinging to his tanned skin.

"I believe you were looking for this." Max smiled, holding out the orange.

"Thanks," Penelope said, mortified that he must have seen her drop everything and then trip and fall into the water.

"Let me get these for you," Max said, moving towards the dropped grocery bags.

Penelope ducked her head to hide her bright red cheeks. "Thanks. I should have made two trips," she said lamely.

"That's Pen for you," Max said as he gathered up the groceries. "Why make two trips when you can take one giant trip?"

"Good one," Penelope said. Two weathered-looking men sat on the back of a boat a few slips down, chuckling as they watched them gather up the bags. Penelope wondered if they would have just watched her drown. "Wait," Penelope said, freezing in place after gathering up the last bag. "What are you really doing here, Max?"

"Arlena got me a part. I'm the newest cast member of *The Yellow Wallpaper*," Max said, heading to the yacht.

"Max, are you bothering Penelope again?" Arlena demanded as the two of them made their way into the main salon of the boat from the front deck.

"What do you mean?" Max said, dimples appearing next to his grin.

"You know what I mean. Leave. Her. Alone." Arlena sat with her long legs folded under her on one of the leather couches that lined the room. Zazoo, her tiny white Bich-Poo, perched on his little red dog bed adjacent to the couch. He lifted his head quickly when they entered, a growl at the back of his throat. The mid-ship level had an open floor plan anchored by the galley on one end and opening into a large living space with club chairs and tea tables throughout, all trimmed in rich leather and oak. "Why are you guys all wet?" Arlena asked, finally noticing something was off about the pair as they made their way through to the galley.

"I saved Penelope's life," Max tossed over his shoulder as they passed.

"Oh good, I can't wait to hear all about it." She rolled her eyes at Max and then said to Penelope, "Are you okay? What happened?"

"I fell in," Penelope said, busying herself with emptying the plastic bags onto the island counter, her cheeks still burning from embarrassment. She pulled open the refrigerator door and slipped all of the packages of meat inside, then started sorting through the vegetables and pantry items.

Arlena walked to the kitchen and put her hand on Penelope's shoulder, turning her gently so they were face to face. She looked into Penelope's eyes then pulled her into a tight hug.

"I'm fine, really," Penelope said. She could feel little drips of water falling from her shorts onto the floor by her feet.

Arlena pulled out of the hug and held Penelope at arm's length, her thin hands placed gently on Penelope's shoulders. "Please be careful, Pen. If anything happened to you, I don't know how I could go on. I need you by my side."

Penelope looked at Arlena, trying to decide how to react. Finally she settled on levity.

"Arlena, nothing is going to happen to me. I promise." She felt like adding "stop being so dramatic" but decided that might be the wrong thing to say. Could you tell a dramatic actress to stop being dramatic? Did it mean the same thing as it did with civilians?

"Sweet, only two of the eggs are cracked. I'll scramble these up now," Max said over his shoulder from the opposite counter. "Anybody else want eggs?"

Arlena held her gaze on Penelope for a second more and then said to Max's back, "Sounds good."

Max scooped some scrambled eggs onto his fork with a piece of bacon.

"What is this part then?" Penelope asked him, taking a bite of the fluffy eggs from her plate. Max was a great cook, especially breakfast food.

"It's quite an illustrious role," Max said, grinning at Arlena across the table. "Man at Party is his name."

Arlena rolled her eyes and chewed. "You have a line, a credit and a paycheck, so don't complain."

Max held his hands up in mock surrender, his fork dangling loosely between two fingers.

"No complaints here," he said. "I appreciate the job. You know me, I never turn down work."

"How is it going on the reality show?" Penelope asked. She'd slipped below deck to her cabin while Max made breakfast, changing into a bikini and tank top and twisting her wet hair into a loose bun on top of her head.

"It's going great," Max said. "Just got word we've been renewed for a second season." He raised his mimosa up to toast his sister, but she just waved him off.

"Are you dating Hannah in real life or is that just for the show?" Arlena asked, leveling her gaze at him.

Max glanced sideways at Penelope and casually replied, "That's just for the show. She's a great girl. You know how these things go."

"How what things go? Fake girlfriends? No, I don't know how that goes," Arlena said, shaking her head at Penelope in disbelief. "I saw you making out with her on one of those gossip websites. Looked pretty real to me."

Max smiled sheepishly. "Oh, that was all for publicity, bought and paid for by the show. The producers set us up at that club, VIP room and bottle service all night. The show's ratings went up after we started *dating*." Max dropped his fork and crooked his fingers into air quotes.

"Is she as wild as her parents?" Arlena asked, cutting her eyes at Penelope. Hannah Devore, one of Max's costars on his reality show, was the daughter of British punk rock royalty Niles Devore and his heroin-chic model wife Chastity Devore.

"I don't know," Max answered innocently. "I've never partied with her parents."

Penelope focused on her plate in an attempt to stay out of the conversation. She'd kissed Max once the previous winter, sort of a spur-of-the-moment decision, and they'd never talked about it since.

"Did the producers pay for the hotel room?" Arlena asked, teasing her brother.

"Of course they did," Max said, digging into his breakfast again. "You think I'd invite a camera crew back to a hotel with me if I was on a real date?"

Arlena sighed. "I suppose not. Just be careful. I wouldn't want my little brother to get his heart broken by some famous floozy."

"Hannah's a nice girl. And who says 'floozy' anymore? Oh, wait, are you using old-timey language to stay in character during filming?"

"You should broaden your vocabulary. And limit the range of women you think are acceptable to date," Arlena scolded, pushing her plate aside and reaching for her mimosa.

Penelope finished eating and murmured "Excuse me" as she stood up to clear her place at the table.

"Pen knows I have wonderful taste in women."

Penelope blushed. "No comment," she said over her shoulder as she busied herself with rinsing her plate and putting it in the dishwasher. "Thanks for breakfast. Not to change the subject or anything, but I got some nice steaks this morning. Maybe we can grill off the back deck later?"

"Perfect," Arlena said.

Max stood up and walked behind Arlena's chair. He leaned down and gave her a hug from behind, one large arm draped around her neck. Arlena nuzzled him back for a moment and then leaned up and kissed his cheek. "I just worry about you, you little twerp," she said, shaking her head at him. "Be careful. Don't be like Daddy and attempt to populate the world on your own, one starlet at a time."

"I wouldn't dream of it, sis," Max said.

CHAPTER 5

Penelope, Max and Arlena left for breakfast together the next morning after spending a leisurely Saturday afternoon and evening on the boat. Penelope felt rested, and had enjoyed the downtime floating out in the ocean, eating, drinking wine and reading over a few scripts with Arlena. She was contemplating her next project, and had brought several with her to consider.

Max offered his arm to the ladies as they stepped off of the yacht and onto the dock. The two old fishermen who had watched Penelope fall into the water the previous morning were out on the back of their boat again. They always seemed to be out there, in the same fraying aluminum deck chairs, wearing beat-up sun visors and staring wordlessly at everyone who walked past them, offering an occasional nod or wave. The only thing that changed with them was their clothes, on occasion, and what type of drink they were holding. If it was morning, it was coffee mugs, and any time after noon it was almost always a beer can.

Something was different about them this morning though. Usually, they smiled benignly, keeping to themselves but acknowledging their dock neighbors. Today they stared more intently, scowling at the group as they passed. Penelope glanced away after her wave was not returned.

"I guess they woke up on the wrong side of the floor this morning," she muttered to herself.

The trio walked up the dock towards the shore, passing the usual boats and more than a few empty slips. When they reached the marina's office, Penelope noticed a boat she'd never seen before rocking gently against the dock. It was a plain white speedboat with big blue letters that spelled POLICE along the sides and back. She pointed it out to Arlena and Max who walked slightly ahead of her, discussing what they might order for breakfast.

Max glanced around at Penelope and the boat.

"Yeah, so?"

"I was just thinking I've never seen a police boat here before," Penelope said. "We've been here a month, and I've never even seen a police officer, now that I think about it."

"We know how much you like police officers, Pen," Max teased.

Penelope took one more look at the boat then quickened her pace to catch up to them. When they stepped onto the sandy walkway that headed to Ocean Avenue, Penelope noticed a definite change in the air, a tension in the faces of the people they passed.

"Which way is this Inn you've been going on about?" Max said, adjusting his reflective sunglasses as he looked up and down the beach. "Where are all the sunbathers? It's a beach, right?"

Arlena scoffed. "This isn't South Beach or Ibiza, Max. Why do you think we're filming a movie that takes place in 1890 here? Shane doesn't want a bunch of random people in neon bikinis in the background. We're practically on a deserted island."

"They do get some tourists," Penelope said, "but we've

sectioned off most of the beach for the shoot. We hardly see anyone who isn't with the production."

They made a right on Ocean Avenue and headed towards The Andrea Island Inn. It sat at the north end of the beach, and was owned by a lovely older woman named Jeanne. Her skin was baked to a wrinkly finish from sitting on the hotel's rooftop deck with her guests, watching the ocean roll in and out for over forty years.

Jeanne told Penelope she had taken over the Inn from her parents, just like they had from her grandparents, who had built the Andrea Inn on the biggest bluff overlooking the ocean. They were one of the original families to settle on the island and are fiercely proud and protective of it. The Inn was indeed impressive, but was starting to show its age, mostly in the thin sheets and worn-around-the-edges comforters on the beds.

The main hallway of the lobby was spacious and stretched from the front of the building out to the rear veranda and the swimming pool that overlooked the ocean. Jeanne kept the wooden double doors on each open during the day to let in the natural light and ocean breeze.

They entered the restaurant and Penelope's heart skipped a beat when she saw two of her chefs sitting at a table in the rear corner talking to a couple of police officers. One of the officers was a large black man, his biceps straining the short sleeves of his pale blue golf shirt as he leaned his elbows on the table. A badge-shaped emblem with the state of Florida in the middle of it was stitched on his shirt, the word POLICE under it in dark blue letters. The other officer was a slender Spanish woman in a matching uniform, her arms folded tightly at her chest.

Francis looked down at his hands clasped loosely in his lap, his head shaking slightly as he listened to the conversation at the table.

Quentin sat up straight, his expression one of concern as he answered the officer's questions.

Jeanne hurried over to the podium to greet them. "Oh good lord, Penelope, I'm so glad you're here. Oh, and Miss Madison and..."

"This is my brother, Max," Arlena said.

"Oh, well," Jeanne said. Her usually serene smile had been replaced with a nervous grimace. She began gathering up various menus, almost dropping them at one point. Her eyes flicked towards the back of the dining room at the table with the police officers. "They've been trying to call you, Penelope. Those detectives are asking about the two young girls you have working for you."

"Why, what's going on?" Penelope asked, alarm sending a red flush up her neck to her cheeks. She pulled her backpack from her shoulders and reached inside for her phone. She had three missed calls, one from an unknown Florida number, one from Francis and one from Joey. "My phone must be on silent. I can't believe I missed all of these calls."

"Nobody knows where the girls are," Jeanne said, lowering her voice and glancing furtively around the room. Her silver curls swayed around her glasses that were always perched on the end of her nose when not swinging by a lanyard around her neck. "Their parents are really upset. They've been up and down the beach looking for them all weekend. No one has seen them."

"That's terrible," Penelope said. "Do you think they crossed over to the mainland?"

"The ferry captain doesn't remember seeing them," Jeanne said, putting the menus in the crook of her elbow and wringing her hands. "The detectives came by this morning, started questioning my guests." Jeanne shook her head. "I'm sorry, dear, let's get you a table."

"I'll be right over," Penelope said to Arlena. "I'm going to check on my guys."

Jeanne led Arlena and Max in the opposite direction to a four top next to the large picture window overlooking the ocean. Penelope weaved her way to the table in the back. A few of the diners eyed her quietly while others gazed curiously at the back table.

"And that was the last time you saw them?" The male detective was directing his question at both of her chefs across the breakfast table. He was making notes in a leather-bound notebook in front of him as they spoke.

"Yes, sir," Francis said. "We all did. It was a big party, and practically everyone from work was there. Hey, Boss," he said as Penelope neared the table.

"You guys okay?" Penelope asked.

Quentin continued to stare at the table.

"This is Detective Williams and Detective Torres," Francis said, nodding towards the other side of the table. "They're looking for Sabena and Rebekkah."

Detective Torres leaned forward.

"And you are?"

"I'm Penelope Sutherland. I'm the head caterer on the movie," Penelope said, extending her hand. Torres stood up rigidly from her seat and shook firmly. Detective Williams stood up and looked down at Penelope, towering over her by at least a foot. He shook her hand with similar authority then retook his seat.

"Miss Sutherland..." Detective Williams said, flipping over a page in his notebook. "We have you on our list of people to talk to. You hired Rebekkah Flores and Sabena Lambert to work as waitresses on the set?"

"Yes. On occasion, we have the girls come and serve for us.

It's usually either for lunch or dinner, no more than twelve to fifteen hours a week."

"How well do you know them?" Detective Torres asked. Her arms had found their way back into a tight fold across her chest.

Penelope thought for a second. "I've only known them for a few weeks. I do know they're best friends. Sabena told me she and Rebekkah have been since they were little."

Detective Williams took notes as she spoke.

"They're hard workers. I've never had an issue with them not showing up or causing any problems during service. Have you tried locating their phones?"

Detective Williams shook his head. "We aren't able to track either phone, which is unusual. It appears they've both been turned off, or the batteries are dead."

"If they decided to go somewhere together for the weekend and they didn't want their parents to find out, they could have just turned them off to avoid being found," Penelope said, hopefully.

"Maybe," Detective Williams said with a note of skepticism, staring at his notepad. "Teenage girls and their phones, though...Miss Sutherland, how did the girls come to work for you?" He glanced up at her.

"I put an ad on Craigslist, an open call for servers who could work flexible hours but nothing permanent or full-time. I just needed a couple of people to fill in for two or three hours here and there when we have a larger service. They came to meet me together and I hired them on the spot. They're sweet girls, and good students, according to their parents. Florida doesn't require me to get work permits for underage hires, but I had them bring me written permission agreements. I remember both of them were signed by their mothers. I can get their employment information for you, those permissions and the hours they've worked." Penelope glanced over her shoulder and saw that Jeanne was filling two mismatched mugs for Max and Arlena, coffee for him and hot water for her.

"That would be helpful, Miss Sutherland," Detective Torres said, pulling a card from her front pocket. "You can email everything to me."

"Sure. I'll do it as soon as possible," Penelope said.

"Can any of you think of anything else that might be helpful?"

Penelope and her chefs all shook their heads. Then Penelope said suddenly, "I saw Sabena's mom Saturday morning at Rose's beach shop on Ocean Avenue. She hadn't heard from Sabena and couldn't reach her on the phone."

Officer Williams flipped back a few pages in his notebook and nodded, then made a quick note and closed it. "Thank you for your time. We might be in touch again, so please stay available."

"We're all here most of the time," Penelope said. "A captive audience on the island."

"That's why it's strange two girls could just up and disappear," Detective Torres said sharply.

"And you're positive they didn't head over to the mainland, lose track of time in Miami or something like that?" Penelope asked.

"Unfortunately no one remembers seeing them together or separately since Friday. There aren't any cameras on the ferry, but there's one in the mainland terminal. We're still reviewing the footage, but so far there's no sign of either of them," Detective Williams said. "They're officially missing persons, critical missing because of their age."

Penelope bent Detective Torres' card lightly between her fingers, glancing down at it. "Of course, if there is anything we can do...any of us," she motioned to her two chefs, "let us know. I hope they turn up soon."

The detectives excused themselves and left the restaurant, stopping to say something to Jeanne at the hostess podium. As they approached the door, a couple entered. Penelope guessed they were Rebekkah's parents from the worried looks on their faces and the resemblance between Rebekkah and the woman.

"Were you able to tell them anything helpful?" Penelope asked, glancing back at her chefs.

"Someone told those detectives Sabena and Rebekkah were drinking at the party," Francis said. "But I swear, Boss, I only saw them drinking water, nothing else." Quentin and Francis both looked relieved that the detectives had left, and a little queasy.

Penelope flicked her eyes towards the door again, and saw the couple talking with the detectives, a nervous Jeanne wringing her hands and listening. "Did you see the girls leave with anyone after the party?" she asked Francis.

"Last I saw, they were with Regan. He said he would make sure they got home okay. They all live in that development off the main avenue, past Rose's. When we left, the party was winding down, but there were still a bunch of people hanging out."

Penelope pictured the development he was talking about. It was the only large cluster of houses on the island, three or four winding streets with modest ranchers that looked like they might have been new in the 1970s. She figured it would be about a fifteen-minute walk from the beach party to where the girls lived.

"Have any of you guys seen Regan this weekend?" Penelope asked, remembering how she had found him early Saturday morning, passed out on the avenue.

"We haven't. The other chefs from our crew went over to the mainland Saturday morning, and they're not back yet," Quentin said, shrugging. "Maybe they know something, but I doubt it."

"You guys didn't want to get off the island with them?" Penelope asked, shifting her weight and adjusting her backpack on her shoulders.

"Nah," Francis said. "We hiked on the other side of the island and camped out Saturday night. Just came back into town for breakfast an hour ago."

Penelope thought for a moment and said, "Do me a favor and call me when the whole team is back on the island. I want to have a meeting with all of us together. In the meantime, keep an eye out for the girls, and let me know if the police want to talk to you again." She smiled reassuringly in response to their worried glances, then walked over to the hostess podium.

"Jeanne," Penelope interrupted.

"Penelope, have you met Rebekkah's parents?" Jeanne said, making the introductions.

Rebekkah's mom looked at her with a confused expression, her face creased with worry. "You're from the movie," Mrs. Flores said, hugging her arms around her chest, her purse strap twisting in the crook of her arm.

"I wanted to let you know, if I can help with anything, please give me a call."

Penelope reached into her backpack and pulled out her business card, handing it to Mrs. Flores. Mr. Flores looked down at Penelope sternly, not offering a hello or and handshake, his face a mask of concern.

"We'll do anything we can to help find them," Penelope said earnestly.

Mr. Flores shook his head and turned abruptly away,

storming back into the hallway of the Inn. Jeanne followed him out, wringing her hands.

"He's upset. We all are," Mrs. Flores said distractedly. Her large brown eyes were glassy and red, and her jaw was set in a firm line under her soft features. "It's not like them to worry us like this. They're good girls."

Penelope nodded. "I know...I really hope they turn up soon. Please call me if you think of anything I can do, or if you need to talk to anyone from the production. I can put you in touch with whoever you need." She pointed out her cell number on the card in Mrs. Flores' hand.

"You know, that's why we let her come to work for you. She earned our trust, never breaking her curfew, keeping up her grades," Mrs. Flores said. "Me and her dad, we both work at the school; we keep a close eye on her."

"It sounds like this is totally out of character for both of them," Penelope said. She thought to herself that wasn't great news. If the girls had a history of running away or breaking curfew, maybe their sudden disappearance wouldn't be as upsetting. Two girls who normally followed the rules vanishing into thin air was harder to explain, and definitely more troubling.

"I have to get home, in case she calls. The police said we should," Mrs. Flores said. She thanked Penelope and followed her husband out into the hallway.

Penelope wound her way over to Arlena and Max's table and took a seat, motioning to a worried-looking Jeanne with her empty coffee mug. She hurried over with a steaming carafe.

"They're in such a state," she said. "Such a nice family, I feel so badly for them."

The table fell silent, as they thought of how to proceed.

"I'll give you another minute or two," Jeanne said, turning

away. She had regained some of her poise, but her hands shook a little more than usual when she poured their coffee.

"A couple of teenagers are missing?" Max asked Penelope after Jeanne had stepped away.

Penelope busied herself fixing her coffee, adding cream until it was just the right color of light brown. "Rebekkah and Sabena, the girls who work for me as servers on set. No one has seen them since Friday night and the police are looking for them."

"How can someone go missing on an island this small?" Arlena asked.

"I'm not sure," Penelope said. "I just met with Rebekkah's parents. They're really worried about her, understandably."

"I talked with Rebekkah the other day after lunch. She has an interest in acting, was talking about starting a drama club over at the school," Arlena said. "Sweet girl...I told her she should do it, form the club. And I offered to go and talk to whoever the teacher would be, see if they wanted any advice. I think she was going to set something up."

"Do either of them have a boat?" Max asked after taking a sip of coffee.

"I've never heard them talking about their families owning boats. But I don't know them all that well either," Penelope said.

"Don't worry, Pen. I'm sure they'll turn up soon. Let's stay positive, and keep an eye out for them," Arlena said. She put her menu down on the table and wrapped her hands around her mug of tea. "Oh look, it's Gavin."

Arlena's costar was in the doorway of the restaurant chatting with Jeanne, still wearing his sunglasses. When he noticed Arlena in the front of the room, he made his way over to their table.

"Good morning, all," he said.

"Have you had breakfast? We have an extra seat," Arlena said.

"Not yet. That would be lovely, thanks," Gavin said.

"Max, this is Gavin McKenna. Gavin, this is my brother Max," Arlena said.

"Max Madison," Gavin said, shaking Max's hand. "It's nice to meet you. I've watched your show." He took the empty seat next to Penelope.

"Good to meet you too," Max said. "I know Arlena is enjoying working with you."

"You're a fan of Max's show? The one with all the children of famous people behaving badly in Lower Manhattan?" Arlena asked, a bit incredulously.

"Yeah, I'm a big fan, it's quite entertaining," Gavin said, removing his sunglasses. "I need coffee."

Penelope winced at his bloodshot eyes.

"Rough night?"

"Yeah, but that was two nights ago. I'm still hungover from Friday. I couldn't even get out of bed yesterday." Gavin looked longingly at his empty coffee mug.

"Whatever you had in that flask got you, huh?" Penelope teased.

Gavin grimaced and shook his head.

"Has everyone decided?" Jeanne asked, suddenly at their tableside again.

They made their breakfast orders, and Jeanne hurried away, stopping first to clear a few dirty plates and mugs from the table next to theirs.

"Have you heard about the missing girls?" Penelope asked.

"What girls?" Gavin asked, busy fixing his coffee.

Penelope filled him in on what she'd learned from the police and her chefs.

"And now they're missing?" Gavin asked, momentarily distracted by something out the window.

"Do you remember seeing Rebekkah or Sabena talking with anyone after we left?"

Gavin sat back in his chair and closed his eyes. He was silent for so long Penelope thought maybe he had dozed off. His eyes snapped open suddenly and he said, "Yes, I do. I was sitting at the bar and they were with that young fellow who has been hanging around the set. The other one who works for you, right? Tall, thin, black hair?"

"Regan?" Penelope asked.

"I suppose so," Gavin said. "He was talking to them and your other chefs, and that loud French guy in the Hawaiian shirt. I was having a drink with Shane at the bar." Gavin grimaced and shook his head. "And honestly after that things get a bit fuzzy. Afterwards a few of the guys from the crew were upstairs in my room, just listening to music and playing cards. I passed out right as the sun was coming up."

"Gavin, you're lucky you had an extra day off to get that out of your system," Arlena said, giving him a stern look.

"We should hang out sometime," Max said with a quick laugh.

"So you didn't see the girls leave the party?" Penelope asked.

"Sorry, love. I can't remember," Gavin said sheepishly. Glancing at Max he said, "A few of us from the crew are going to Josie's tonight. It will be a more mellow evening than Friday was, for sure. They're having a local band in if you want to join us, meet some of your new coworkers."

"Sure, thanks," Max said.

Arlena wrinkled her nose. "That place is crawling with shellfish."

"It is called Josie's Shrimp Shack. They're not trying to be discreet about it," Gavin said.

Just then a young waiter came over to their table, a large oval tray on his shoulder. He placed their breakfasts down in front of them, pancakes for the guys and egg white veggie omelets for the ladies.

"Could I get a fill up when you get a chance?" asked Gavin.

The waiter smiled shyly. "Of course. Be right back."

"I love it here," Gavin said, forking a big bite of pancake into his mouth. "Everyone is so nice. I could move into the Andrea Inn and be happy for the rest of my days. It's our own private paradise, isn't it?"

Penelope stared at her plate and thought that it wasn't a very happy paradise for Rebekkah and Sabena's families, not at the moment at least.

"It's good you're enjoying your time here," Arlena said.

"It's nice to be somewhere warm where it's not constantly raining," Gavin said cheerfully. "It's heavenly, being in the tropics, not having to put on a bunch of layers. And you can't beat the smell of the ocean."

Penelope tried to focus on the conversation, but her mind kept wandering back to the last time she saw the girls, and to finding Regan in the state he was in on Saturday morning. She ate her breakfast without really tasting it as she went over it again and again. Her stomach began to tighten with worry and dread.

CHAPTER 6

Arlena, Max and Penelope said goodbye to Gavin in the lobby of the Inn and walked out the front door to Ocean Avenue. As they headed back towards the marina, Penelope noticed a commotion in front of the empty building next to Sackler's Market.

"There's those cops again," Max said. "Who's the punk rocker?"

Penelope squinted and put her hand up to shade her eyes. "That's Emilio Babineau, my old chef instructor."

Penelope saw Detective Williams standing next to Emilio with his hands on his gun belt, nodding as Emilio spoke.

"I wonder what's going on," Penelope said.

"They're probably asking him the same questions they asked you," Arlena said. "He was at the party too, and Gavin said he saw the girls talking to him."

As they got closer Penelope began to overhear their conversation. The three of them paused a few feet away, watching Emilio from behind as the detectives questioned him.

"...zoning approved the remodel last week and the construction crew is coming over on Monday," Emilio said. "I've been on the other side of the island at my house all weekend, which is another renovation site. I'm up to my ears with everything going on, getting permits, setting up meetings, trying to get both of these projects underway."

"Can anyone confirm your whereabouts on Friday night?" Detective Torres asked sharply.

"My wife," Emilio said quickly. "I called her from the house after I got home from the party. I'm sorry those girls are missing, I really am, but I had nothing to do with it. You can check. I've been with people all weekend. I had lunch Saturday afternoon with Shane Guthrie. He picked me up at the house...he can tell you no girls were there."

"We'll be looking into all of that," Detective Williams said. "We've heard from several people that you were talking with Rebekkah and Sabena at the party. Did either of them say anything to you about running away or going to the mainland for the weekend?"

"Not that I remember," Emilio said, relaxing a bit. "They were having fun, from what I could tell."

"Did you see them drinking alcohol on the beach?" Detective Williams asked. His deep voice was calm and soothing, which didn't fit with his serious expression.

Emilio held his palms up, fending off the question. "They didn't get any from me, I swear."

"Is this your vehicle?" Detective Torres asked, eyeing a white double cab pickup truck with an enclosed camper shell, the Craw Daddy's logo blazed across both sides.

Penelope turned to Arlena and Max, then urged them to follow her.

"I'm going to say something to him," Penelope said. They walked out onto the street around the truck and stood near it to continue watching the conversation.

Emilio looked at the truck and said, "I bought it for the restaurant."

Detective Torres walked around the truck and looked in the cab's windows. "You mind if we take a look inside?"

"Don't you need a warrant for that?" Emilio asked.

Penelope looked at Emilio quickly, his expression a mix of apprehension and resignation.

"Sure, we can go back to the station and get a warrant, but that will take time," Officer Williams soothed. "Time those girls might not have. Don't you want to help us find them? It's part of our search, looking at all of the enclosed vehicles on the island." The large man nodded reassuringly as he spoke.

Emilio looked at his boots, then said, "Sure, take a look. I have nothing to hide."

"We appreciate that, Mr. Babineau," Officer Torres said, not sounding very appreciative.

"I guess if it helps," Emilio mumbled as he dug in his pocket for the keys. He clicked the fob to unlock the front doors, then walked behind the truck and opened the cab's window, swinging it up and then lowering the rear gate. He stepped away and Detective Torres pulled a thin flashlight from her utility belt, twisting it on and shining the beam inside the rear of the truck.

Penelope took a few steps closer and said, "Hi, Chef. Everything okay?"

"Penelope," Emilio said, relief flooding his face. "Detectives, this is Penelope Sutherland, my former student. She can tell you I had nothing to do with those girls going missing."

"Hello again, Miss Sutherland," Officer Williams said. "Were you with Mr. Babineau on Friday night?"

Penelope stammered, "Yes, at the party. I'm sure Emilio wouldn't do anything—"

"Of course I wouldn't. You saw me, I was with Shane. We threw the party together. I talked with lots of people there," Emilio rambled, his words coming faster the more he spoke.

"You were one of the last people seen with the girls," Detective Williams said. "We have a witness who says the party had broken up and afterwards you were talking with Sabena, Rebekkah and..." he consulted his notepad, "Regan Daniels."

"But there were other people around. If someone saw us talking, someone else had to have been there too."

Detective Torres pulled on a pair of latex gloves and hoisted herself onto the rear gate of the truck. She squatted and duck-walked into the camper, her rubber-soled boots squeaking along the bed of the truck as she moved farther in.

Penelope glanced around and noticed all of the little houses nearby had at least one person outside on the porch, watching the drama unfold.

"Is this yours?" Detective Torres asked. She crouched on the back of the truck holding a small silver purse in her hand.

Penelope's stomach dropped when she recognized the purse that had been draped across Rebekkah at the beach party.

"I have no idea how that got there. Maybe it's my wife's," Emilio said, looking curiously at the purse.

Detective Torres snapped it open and looked inside, gently sorting through the contents with a latex-covered finger. After a few seconds she pulled out a laminated card and held it up. Rebekkah smiled at them from the front of her student ID.

Emilio seemed to fold in on himself, his shoulders dipping towards his chest.

"How do you explain Rebekkah Flores's purse in the back of your truck?" Detective Torres asked, closing the purse and leveling her gaze at him.

"I can't," Emilio said. "And I can't help you with anything else. I'm sorry they're gone, but I didn't do anything. It wasn't me, and I have no idea how her purse got back there."

Detective Williams and Torres stepped aside, conferring

with each other in hushed voices. Detective Torres pulled out her phone after a few seconds and made a call.

Emilio looked at Penelope hopefully and lowered his voice. "Penelope, you have to back me up on this."

Penelope shook her head, trying to understand what was happening. "Chef, when did you last see the girls? How did Rebekkah's purse get in the back of your truck?"

"I have no idea. It's been parked in the driveway at the house since Friday."

"Then what is there to back you up on?" Penelope said.

"Pen?" Arlena called from where she and Max stood behind them on the sidewalk. "Is everything okay?"

Penelope flicked a gaze at Arlena over her shoulder. "I'm not sure." Turning back to Emilio she said, "You went home after the party, right?"

Emilio hesitated before saying, "Yes, of course."

"Chef, what happened? Were you talking with Sabena and Rebekkah after the party broke up like they're saying?"

Emilio's expression closed, and he took a step away from her. "I shouldn't be saying anything to anyone. Do me a favor, Penelope, if they ask you about me, tell them I'm a good person and I wouldn't hurt those girls."

Penelope suddenly felt nauseous. "Chef, what about the thing that happened at school? What if they start looking into your past?"

"Nothing happened at school," Emilio said quickly. He grabbed Penelope's forearm with his thick fingers, pressing into her skin. "No charges were filed, and the girls recanted their stories to the dean. I was set up by those little...never mind."

"But you left school because of what happened, in the middle of the term," Penelope said, twisting from under his grip. Red slashes in the shape of his fingers circled her arm. Arlena stepped up behind Penelope and shot a warning glance at Emilio.

"I left because it was time for me to go," Emilio said harshly. "It was part of the settlement, and it was the best thing for everyone, including me. I never touched those girls, and they know it."

"Mr. Babineau," Officer Torres interrupted, clipping her phone back onto her belt. "We'd like you to come with us and answer some more questions."

Emilio started shaking his head before she was finished talking. "I don't think so. Unless I'm under arrest, I'm finished helping you." The word "helping" dripped with sarcasm.

"Have it your way," Officer Torres said crisply. "We're getting warrants to search your properties, so we'll be seeing you again very soon." Officer Williams stood behind her, his hands on his waist.

"If you have anything more to tell us, now would be the time," Officer Williams said in a gentle tone. "These are just kids, remember."

Emilio shook his head again as he turned away from them. "I'm sorry," he whispered to Penelope.

"Are you okay?" Arlena asked, rubbing the red spots on Penelope's arm.

"I guess," Penelope said, still a bit stunned.

Max excused himself and went to Sackler's to pick up some groceries before they headed back to the boat.

"I know he's your former teacher and everything, but he seems like a jerk, Pen," Arlena said with concern after Max left.

Penelope put her hand on her hips and looked at the sidewalk, going back over their conversation in her mind.

"What were you talking about, the thing at school?" Arlena asked.

Penelope looked up and said, "He left his position teaching at culinary school because two students came forward and said he was inappropriate with them in the kitchen and after hours. One of them said they had a sexual relationship, at least that's what I heard."

"Those are serious accusations," Arlena said sharply.

"I know, it was bad," Penelope said quickly. "But eventually both girls withdrew their complaints. He had already resigned as part of a settlement with the school and the students involved."

"Were these underage girls?" Arlena asked.

Penelope shook her head. "No, culinary school is like college, students are all ages. Some of the students are young, like I was, right out of high school. Both of the girls involved were in my track, and roughly my age, so maybe twenty at the time."

"What was the issue, then?" Arlena asked.

"The school has a policy against chef instructors fraternizing with students. Which is funny, in a way. I went out to dinner all the time with my teachers, usually in a group, and we talked about the food and wine, like an extension of what we were learning in the kitchens. I think the line is easy to cross, you know? The nature of the craft is social."

"You said it was two female students. Maybe he has a thing for young girls," Arlena said.

"Maybe," Penelope said, holding her palms up weakly and shrugging. "He was exonerated back then. I hate to think the same kind of thing is happening to him again, or worse, all of it is true."

Arlena's face set in a stern frown. "You have to wonder

about someone getting into similar trouble more than once. He's the common factor in both situations."

Penelope nodded, worry twisting her stomach. "I always thought it was odd, thinking back about what happened at school. One day he was there and the next day he was gone. And the two students who accused him weren't anything alike, weren't friends, not that I remember. I wondered about them plotting against him with each other, but it didn't seem realistic at the time."

"Why do you say that?" Arlena asked.

"I don't know. I just could never work it out in my mind. After Emilio left, I tried to put the rumors about him out of my mind and just focus on graduating. Things were different at the school; the other instructors kept their distance, the atmosphere had changed."

Max walked back over to them, a grocery bag dangling from his hand.

"Come on, let's head back to the boat," Arlena said.

"You guys go ahead," Penelope said. She straightened her shoulders and adjusted her backpack straps. "I want to see if I can find Sabena's mom, try and think of a way to help."

"Are you sure?" Arlena asked, concern pinching her face. "The police are doing everything they can to find the girls, Pen."

"I know. I just need to do something to help, or I'm going to go nuts. I feel like part of this is my fault. I left them at the party. I should have kept better watch over them, offered them a ride home. I didn't do enough to protect them."

"Pen, you're their boss, not their mother," Max said, placing a hand on her shoulder. "Don't be so hard on yourself."

Penelope hesitated for a moment, then shook her head. "No, I won't be able to stop thinking about it if I don't try and help. I'll catch up with you guys in a little while."

Penelope watched Max and Arlena walk back towards the docks, then saw Henny Sackler outside her grocery store, bending over to refill the crates of fruit on the front porch. When she saw Penelope's shadow approaching from behind her, she stood up and turned around quickly.

"Penelope, nice to see you," Henny said warmly. She dropped her voice a notch and said, "I saw you talking with those detectives, and that new fellow." She looked over Penelope's shoulder at the sidewalk where Emilio and the detectives had been. Penelope looked too, and noticed many of the neighbors had remained on their porches, a few of them still gazing at the Craw Daddy's truck.

"Have the police talked to you yet?" Penelope asked.

"Oh, yes. You know, I think they're questioning everyone. I'm sorry to say I have no idea where those girls might be. When I heard they went missing late Friday night...well, I'm in bed by nine. Early hours at the store, you know. I'm afraid I'm no help with anything that happens later than that around here."

"Do you know the girls?"

"Oh, yes. I've been on the island my whole life. It's safe to say I know just about everyone."

An older man in faded swimming trunks walked toward them from the parking lot. He removed his straw hat and bowed slightly to Henny. "How you doing, Henny? I'm here for my weekly order," he said through gapped teeth. Henny said goodbye to Penelope quickly and ushered him inside.

Penelope stood still for a moment, deciding her next move. She selected a few oranges and grapefruits from the crates, and placed them in a sun-bleached shopping basket.

CHAPTER 7

Penelope walked up Ocean Avenue, a paper shopping bag from Sackler's swinging from her hand. The sun beat down on the top of her head and she thought about the hat on the counter in her bathroom back on the yacht.

She made a left on Seafoam Avenue and slowed her pace, squinting at the numbers on the weathered mailboxes as she walked. At the end of the cul-de-sac, she knocked on the door of number twelve, grateful for the shade the small porch provided. The house was faded green with beech-wood shutters, and the front window rattled slightly when Mrs. Lambert pulled the door open. Her eyes were bloodshot and puffy, her expression a mix of fear and hopefulness. She squinted at Penelope through the dirty screen door and her mouth fell open, but she said nothing.

"Mrs. Lambert," Penelope said, "I..." Penelope suddenly forgot what she had practiced saying on the walk over.

Mrs. Lambert continued to stare at her through the screen.

Penelope hoisted up the bag, offering it to the stunned woman. "I brought some groceries. I wasn't sure what—"

"Penelope," Mrs. Lambert said, as if waking up from a dream. She swung the door outward, the squeaking hinges sounding loudly in the damp air. "Come in."

Penelope stepped inside, momentarily blinded by the dark interior of the living room. Mrs. Lambert shuffled behind her, picking up a remote and muting the large flat screen television that teetered on a too-small cabinet in the corner of the room. A doorway next to it led to the kitchen and Penelope went through, placing the grocery bag on the counter, pushing aside a stack of bills and junk mail. She looked back through the doorway and saw Mrs. Lambert was sitting on the couch, staring at the television, a cordless phone lying in her lap.

"I picked up a few things for you," Penelope said tentatively. "Some fruit and a rotisserie chicken from Sackler's."

Mrs. Lambert looked away from the television and at Penelope standing in the kitchen doorway. "I'm not supposed to leave the house, in case Bean calls." She looked down at the dingy white phone in her lap, willing it to ring. Her eyes slid back to the television, focusing on a twenty-four-hour news channel. Tickers sped across the bottom of the screen, announcing news from places in the world far away from Andrea Island.

Penelope paused a moment, concerned that whatever she might say would be the wrong thing. "Can I do anything for you?" she finally asked.

Mrs. Lambert shook her head slowly at the television. "Bean is a good girl. She always calls when she's going to be out late. Never any problems."

"Is there anyone who can come and be with you while you wait?" Penelope asked.

"I do everything on my own," Mrs. Lambert said dreamily. Penelope's eyes flicked to a prescription bottle next to a box of tissues on the end table beside her.

"Are you sure you don't want to call someone from your family? Maybe Sabena is with—"

Mrs. Lambert let out a quick laugh, the first time she seemed not in a daze. "I already called her dad. He's in Vermont. He was no good to us when he was around, but he's decent enough to let me know if she'd turned up there. He can't be bothered with us." She sighed and sank back against the couch.

Penelope glanced down the hallway off the living room. "Can I use your bathroom?"

Mrs. Lambert nodded and waved lazily behind her, unmuting the television. News of a natural disaster somewhere far away echoed off the bare walls of the living room.

Penelope closed the door behind her and washed her hands in the pink porcelain sink, dabbing a few drops of water on her forehead. The noise from the television increased, and she could hear the news report clearly through the door. She looked at the faded pink, bleach-stained towels hanging behind her and decided to air dry her hands, since they looked like they hadn't been washed recently. She pulled aside the shower curtain, exposing the vintage pink porcelain tub. The grout was wearing away in a few spots, but it was relatively clean. She popped open the mirrored door of the medicine cabinet and poked through a few pill vials, recognizing the names of a few anti-anxiety medicines, their names familiar from commercials she'd seen.

The phone rang on the other side of the door and Penelope jumped, closing the medicine cabinet with a snap. She stepped out into the hallway and looked at the back of Mrs. Lambert's head over the couch as she spoke on the phone.

"No, nothing yet," Mrs. Lambert said, her voice breaking at the end. She began to nod as she listened to someone on the phone, and then she started to cry, grabbing a handful of tissues from the box next to her. "I am...I will..." she said wetly, answering the tinny voice on the other end.

Penelope looked back down the hallway at two bedroom

doors, slightly ajar and facing each other. The one on the left was decorated with sparkly blue and white letters, spelling out Sabena's name. Mrs. Lambert continued to talk on the phone while Penelope slipped down the hall and into the girl's bedroom.

Sabena's bed was made, the thin comforter pulled tight and tucked under her pillow. The walls were covered in posters, a collage of familiar musicians and athletes. A collection of trophies and a pink jewelry box with a ballerina dancing across the lid sat on top of a small bookcase next to the desk. Penelope eased open the jewelry box, which held a few imitation gold necklaces, several sets of stud earrings and Sabena's class ring, a thick silver band with a blue gem in the middle.

Penelope slid open the folding closet doors. Sabena's clothes hung on matching white hangers and two rows of shoes were lined up on the floor. A collection of stuffed bears stared down from a shelf above the hangers next to a short pile of sweatshirts, folded and stacked neatly in the center. Penelope stepped up on her toes and looked further back on the shelf, noticing a box with a small gold latch on it that had been pushed against the wall.

Penelope glanced at the bedroom door, still hearing the loud television and one side of Mrs. Lambert's conversation from the other room. She reached up and pulled the box towards her, almost toppling the sweatshirts onto the floor in the process. Penelope propped the box in the crook of her arm and eased open the top, two silky ribbons in the corners stretching tautly between the box and the lid. An envelope was on top, torn open at the seam. Penelope plucked it out, then walked over to Sabena's desk and placed the box on it to get a better look. She peered inside and saw it was a form letter from the University of Florida, thanking Sabena for her interest in the school and directing her to different websites to get more information about enrolling. Penelope tucked the letter back inside the envelope and looked through the other contents of the box.

Several photographs were stacked together, the first one of two girls around six years old, one with dark hair and one white blond in matching bikinis, fingers linked in front of a plastic wading pool. Penelope smiled when she recognized Sabena and Rebekkah squinting into the camera, the sun shining brightly on their little faces. Rebekkah was missing a front tooth and Sabena had hooked a finger in the side of her mouth, pulling a face at the photographer. Penelope recognized Mrs. Lambert in the next photo sitting next to a man, who she assumed was Sabena's father, on what looked like the same beige couch that was out in the living room. They appeared to be close to Sabena's age now in the photograph, two kids looking uncomfortable and stiff with small smiles on their faces.

As Penelope looked through the photos, an odd smell rose up, a sharp tinge of something burnt. Penelope crinkled her nose and pushed aside a stack of school achievement certificates, finding a plastic bag at the bottom, the top zipped closed. Penelope picked up the bag, looking through the plastic at a charred piece of material and some ripped photographs. She glanced again at the door and opened the bag, the smell of charred fabric hitting her nose immediately. She pulled out the scrap of material, seeing that it was burned the whole way around, as if it had been rescued at the last minute before disappearing into ash. It was thick polyester, dingy white with blue stripes. There were torn threads sticking up from the material, as if something had been ripped from it, in the shape of two letters: A and C.

Penelope looked at the material a few more seconds, then

focused on the photographs inside the bag. There were about half a dozen, all of them ripped or burned, with only Sabena left in the remnants. Penelope plucked one of the halves from the bag, a picture of Sabena coyly eyeing the camera to the right of a jagged rip. She was on the beach at night, the dark ocean water visible behind her. Penelope shook the plastic bag gently to shuffle the pieces of photos but could tell the other half wasn't inside. A man's arm lay lightly across her back, his index finger slipped under the strap of the bathing suit strap on her left shoulder. Penelope held the picture closer, looking for any rings or other distinguishing features.

"What are you doing?" Mrs. Lambert said from the doorway.

Penelope jumped and dropped the photo and plastic bag on the floor. Mrs. Lambert eyed her wearily, bringing a wad of tissues up to her nose.

"Nothing, just looking for something that might help us find the girls," Penelope said, quickly snatching up the bag and replacing all the items in the box.

"Did you find anything?" Mrs. Lambert asked curiously as she wandered over to the desk.

"Maybe. Does Sabena have a boyfriend?" Penelope asked.

"No," Mrs. Lambert answered quickly. "She's not allowed. School comes first, she knows that."

"She's not allowed to date?"

"Not until senior year," Mrs. Lambert said, clearing her throat. "And even then...there's plenty of time for all of that, but for now she's way too young. Why?"

Penelope plucked the plastic bag from the box and showed her the ripped pictures. "Looks like she was trying to cut someone out of her life. Who is this?" Penelope asked, pointing to the picture with the man's hand.

"Sabena's got a lot of friends, boys and girls, always has. She's very well-liked, a student athlete." Mrs. Lambert laughed weakly and rolled her eyes. "I asked her about these, caught her looking through them one night after she was supposed to be in bed. She got into a beef with another girl on her volleyball team at school. The girl graduated and went off to college last year. I told the detectives about it when they found these." She tucked the picture back in the bag and closed the box. "You know how kids are, best friends one minute, mortal enemies the next. Luckily she and Rebekkah have always been like sisters. That was her mom on the phone, checking in."

Penelope looked at the box, and folded her arms across her chest.

"I appreciate you stopping by. That was real nice of you. I'm going to lie down for a while," Mrs. Lambert said, swaying slightly on her feet.

"Of course. If there's anything—"

"I know. That's what everyone says," Mrs. Lambert said, a sharp edge in her voice. "Everyone wants to help. But that's not bringing my baby back to me, is it?"

CHAPTER 8

Penelope walked back down Ocean Avenue, the thick wet air making it hard to pull in a breath. She kept thinking about that hand on Sabena's shoulder, the familiarity of the touch beneath her strap, the look on Sabena's face, trying to act so grown up when she had yet to shake all of the childlike features from the photo when she was just a little girl, playing in the yard with her best friend.

As she got closer to the docks she saw Detectives Torres and Williams again, in the same spot she had left them earlier, outside the vacant building next to Sackler's market. She quickened her step when she saw Emilio also.

"Okay, Mr. Babineau, open it up," Detective Torres ordered, nodding at the frosted glass on the front doors of the vacant building. They were secured with a thick chain and a large padlock.

Emilio tucked a stack of papers they had given him into his back pocket and pulled out his keys. He shrugged and unlocked the padlock. "You're not going to find anything. This place has been locked up tight since last week." When the lock snapped open, he pulled the chain from the doors and swung the left one open.

"Stay put," Detective Torres warned him. She entered the

building, Detective Williams right behind her. The door swished closed behind them.

"Penelope," Emilio said when he saw her approaching. "I called my lawyer. They have a warrant."

"That's good. They'll search your house and the restaurant site, then they'll move on to someone else when they don't find anything."

"It will be a relief. I can't believe this happened on the one weekend I come down here and mix with the locals. I hope that's not an indication of how things are going to go—"

The doors banged open and Detective Williams rushed out, speaking urgently into his cell phone. "We need the chopper. MediVac stat. We've got two unresponsive females, possible OD. We're at Ocean Avenue on Andrea Island, adjacent to Sackler's Market."

Penelope's stomach did a flip and she stepped away from Emilio. He searched her face helplessly as Detective Williams said, "Mr. Babineau, we're placing you under arrest."

The detective's voice faded away in Penelope's mind as she took another step back and stared at her former teacher. His expression morphed from panic to fear to resignation as his hands were cuffed behind his back.

"Penelope," Emilio pleaded as she continued to back away. "I didn't do this."

Penelope stood in the parking lot of Sackler's Market as the MediVac helicopter took off from the athletic field behind the Andrea Island school complex, a small group of stucco buildings that housed the elementary, middle and high schools. After they'd handcuffed Emilio, the detectives sat him down on the sidewalk and re-cuffed him to the base of a sign that read

Andrea Island Historic District in gold letters, his arms lying loosely behind him. Detectives Torres and Williams ushered the EMTs into the vacant building and, moments later, two stretchers came bouncing out, white sheets draped over Rebekkah and Sabena. Penelope caught a glimpse of Sabena's face and her heart sank when she saw the grayish tint to her skin. Penelope closed her eyes, fighting back tears as they passed by.

After several minutes, Penelope went to Emilio and crouched down to talk to him. Detective Williams stood nearby, talking urgently with someone on his phone while Detective Torres draped police tape over the front doors of the restaurant site.

"Penelope, please," Emilio said to her, his eyes slightly wild. "You have to believe me. I had nothing to do with this."

Penelope looked at him closely, swallowing down the sour bile in the back of her throat. "I want to believe you, Chef. But the purse in your truck...and how did the girls get inside your restaurant?"

"I wish I knew. Help me, please," he begged.

"I don't know how to help you," Penelope said, choking on the last word.

"Please, can you do one thing for me? Take the papers from the inside of my jacket and bring them to my house. My wife Dominique is there. It's the permits and other documents for the restaurant. I don't want them to get lost if I'm processed."

Penelope looked at him doubtfully.

"You're the only person on this island who I can trust. And you have nothing to do with this restaurant. I'm still working on everything with the city council. I don't want them to see all of our proposed plans yet. Please, it would be easier. I know it's a lot to ask. I'll owe you one, okay?"

Penelope felt sorry for her once proud and cocky chef instructor, realizing how humiliating all of this must be for him. She also remembered how he patiently gave her special instruction in the kitchen classroom when she'd asked for help to perfect her filleting technique, coming in early on his own time to help her all those years ago. She tried to hold onto that image of him and not the one in front of her now.

"Sure. I can do that for you, Chef." Penelope reached inside his jacket and retrieved a thick fold of papers from the interior pocket.

"Thanks, Penelope. And tell Dominique I'll call. That I'll be home soon," Emilio said. "We're renovating one of the old mansions on the west side of the island, house number four. Just follow Ocean Avenue until it turns into Mangrove Loop. You can't miss it."

"Okay, Mr. Babineau," Detective Williams said, finishing his phone call. "We're taking you over to the mainland station. Let's go." Detectives Williams and Torres led Emilio toward the docks.

Penelope tucked Emilio's paperwork into her backpack, slung it over her shoulders and followed them at a distance. The midday ferry had arrived, its low horn sounding as it began to pull away from the dock and head back to the mainland.

When she reached the marina, Penelope stopped short, her heart making a sudden leap.

Leaning on the railing with his phone up to his ear was Joey, looking her way behind reflective sunglasses, a rolling suitcase propped against his leg. Penelope felt her phone buzzing in her backpack and quickly pulled it from her shoulders. Realizing that was silly, she walked quickly towards him and threw her arms around his neck. He pulled the phone from his ear and hugged her back.

"What're you doing here?" Penelope asked, pulling out of the hug and looking up into his handsome face.

"I came to surprise you. Are you surprised?" Joey asked. "I hope you're surprised and not weirded out. I tried to call, but..."

Penelope kissed him then, stopping him from saying anything else.

CHAPTER 9

"I can't believe you're here," Penelope said after breaking the kiss.

"I have this vacation time I'm going to lose if I don't take, so I decided to come down and see Florida. And you," Joey said, searching her face. "I called this morning when I landed in Miami. I hope you're okay with me just showing up." He hesitated, nervously awaiting her response.

"Yes, of course," Penelope said, finally letting go of him. She linked her fingers in his and smiled. "This is a wonderful surprise."

"I rented a cabin for the week on the south end of the beach, wherever that is," Joey said.

"I'll help you find it. I was just heading to the boat to get my things. Do you want to come and say hi to Arlena?"

"Sure. Hey, I just saw two officers hustling a guy in handcuffs onto a police boat over there," Joey said, pointing at the now empty slip. "I thought you said this was a sleepy little island."

"I know that guy, actually. I have for a long time," Penelope said quietly, looking away from him.

"Oh, sorry," Joey said sheepishly. "What happened?"

"It's a long story," Penelope said. "I'll fill you in when we get to the boat."

Joey took Penelope's hand and led her down the dock, his suitcase bouncing across the warped boards. When they passed the old fishermen, Penelope noticed they were still scowling, but with less menace. They must've moved on to the drinking portion of the day.

When they entered the main salon of the boat, Arlena and Max greeted Joey warmly and invited him to stay. Penelope removed her backpack and sat down on the nearest couch, motioning for Joey to sit next to her. Max offered beers to everyone, and Joey happily accepted.

Joey twisted the cap and took a sip. "Now my vacation can start."

Penelope pulled Emilio's papers from her bag and started to open them, then wondered if she should.

"What's that?" Joey asked, eyeing the paperwork.

"That guy you saw? He was one of my teachers back in culinary school. He just got arrested and asked me to take these papers to his wife on the other side of the island as a favor."

"What is it?" Max asked, leaning against the galley island.

"I think it's the contract for the restaurant building. Maybe the building permits and plans, financial information he didn't want the city council to see. He insisted I take it to her."

"I'll go with you," Joey said. "What was the guy arrested for? Violating building codes?"

"Kidnapping two teenage girls," Penelope said quietly.

Joey's beer bottle stopped halfway to his mouth and he turned to look at her. "Seriously? What's going on around here?"

"He says he didn't do it," Penelope said quickly. "I want to believe him, give him the benefit of the doubt. I think he deserves it."

Joey eyed her tenderly and said, "Sounds like you're got history. You really want to help him, Penny?"

"I think so, yeah," Penelope said, unsure herself. "He just wants me to take this to her. It's not like he's asking me to testify on his behalf or anything."

"Not yet," Arlena chimed in.

"What evidence do they have on him?" Joey asked.

Penelope caught Joey up on everything they had just seen, including finding the purse in Emilio's truck.

"Sounds like he's up against it, Penny. The girls were found alive?"

"As far as I know," Penelope said. She glanced at the paperwork in her hands and unfolded the top portion. She saw *Transfer of Deed* printed at in the header in swirly letters. Emilio's name was typed onto the buyer's line with the name Elizabeth Haverford on the seller line.

"Sometimes innocent people appear guilty, even when they're not," Penelope said, standing up from the couch and heading to the galley. She pulled open the refrigerator and took out a bottle of water.

"Hopefully he's telling the truth and he really had nothing to do with this," Joey said, finishing his beer. Max held up his bottle to offer him another but Joey declined with a wave. "You believe this guy, and that's good enough for me. Let's go deliver the papers to his wife and then we can start enjoying the first day of my vacation."

CHAPTER 10

Penelope called the head of transportation to see if they could borrow one of the production vehicles, then she and Joey went to store his suitcase in her stateroom.

"You're sure you don't mind me just showing up like this, Penny Blue?" Joey asked, calling her by the nickname she'd been given in grade school where they had first met.

Penelope sat on the bed and patted the mattress next to her. "Joey, I'm really glad you're here. I've missed you."

Sitting next to her, he said, "I've missed you too." He leaned in for a kiss. Penelope kissed him back, looping her arms around his neck. Joey's hand slid up her thigh and he shifted back slightly onto the bed, pulling Penelope with him.

"I think the car is probably here by now," Penelope said between kisses, pushing him away gently. Joey groaned and hugged her tighter.

"It will be there whenever we're ready to go," Penelope said. "But I'm afraid if we start something now, I'm never going to want to leave this room."

Joey laughed and kissed her on the forehead. "You're right. Let's get going before I change my mind and lock that door."

A black Range Rover was waiting for them in the first spot at the marina, the keys tucked under the visor.

"Wow, very trusting," Joey said as he climbed into the driver's seat. Penelope buckled up, placing her backpack between her feet on the floor.

"I told him he could leave the keys at the marina office, but he said the truck would be safe out here. I guess it'd be pretty easy to catch a car thief in a place like this."

"Do they take cars back and forth on the ferry?" Joey asked. "I didn't see any on my trip over."

"It's very limited. You have to be issued a permit from the city council, and they only allow a certain number over at a time. Shane had to get special permission for us to bring a few trucks like these for the crew and my three catering trucks. It held up the start of production for a couple of weeks, trying to get the approvals from the Andrea Island powers that be."

"Wow, they run a tight ship down here," Joey said, starting up the truck.

"The ferry only transports cars from the island on Sundays. They don't want a bunch of tourists and their cars on the island; something about protecting the local vegetation and limiting wear and tear on the roads. Makes sense, I suppose."

"I guess if the draw of your island is 'Rustic Old Florida' you'd better deliver. Good for them," Joey said. "Which way am I going?"

"Head up to the avenue and go left. The main road is just a big circle around the island. Emilio said his house is on the other side of the loop."

They opened all the windows and the sunroof and drove to Emilio's. Penelope closed her eyes and breathed in the salty air, feeling relaxed for the first time since her emotional morning.

*   *   *

House number four on Mangrove Loop was a narrow two-story with washed out greenish-blue wooden slats and ornate shutters matching the wraparound porch railings. The roof was covered with large inlaid tiles in a diamond design that must have once been quite grand but was now faded from the sun and the elements. Penelope noticed several of the tiles were cracked or missing altogether. Weathered yellow wooden shutters in the windows were open to let in fresh air. Stepping onto the creaking porch, Penelope noticed the large picture window facing the great room was cracked on one side and held in by blue construction tape. In the corner of the porch where a hanging swing might go was a pile of building supplies, including several boxes of roofing tiles, a few five-gallon paint buckets and some drop cloths.

Penelope used the heavy antique knocker to signal their arrival. When the door opened, Penelope found herself looking straight into the prettiest green eyes she'd ever seen. Dominique Babineau was as petite as Penelope, both reaching just over five feet.

"Can I help you?" Dominique asked, smiling shyly at Penelope.

"Are you Dominique?" Penelope asked hesitantly. She wondered if Dominique knew about Emilio yet. She didn't appear at all distressed.

"Yes, that's me. And you are?" she asked, her eyes drifting over Penelope's shoulder to rest on Joey's face.

"I'm Penelope Sutherland and this is Joseph Baglioni. Emilio was my teacher," Penelope said, glancing back at Joey. "He asked me to bring you something. Have you talked to him recently?"

"Dommie, who is it?" a man's high-pitched voice called from the back of the house. Penelope recognized it immediately, having heard it squeaking nonstop from the walkie-talkie permanently attached to her hip during filming.

"It's some friends of Emilio's," she called over her shoulder. She looked back at them and smiled. "Come in." She opened the door wider and stepped back into the foyer, her bare feet tiny and dark against the big white tiles. She swept her arm to direct them to the back of the house, past a sagging staircase on the right and a small sitting room with inlaid bookshelves on their left.

"Penelope, what are you doing here?" Shane Guthrie said to them as they entered the kitchen. He was sitting on a stool at the kitchen island, his pale, thin hand draped loosely around a coffee mug on the counter. Several sections of the newspaper were spread out on the island and the sink was full of dirty dishes.

Penelope stammered, "We're, um...we're here to drop off something for Emilio. He asked me to bring these." She pulled her backpack from her shoulders and retrieved the paperwork. Dominique watched her quietly, leaning her hip against the kitchen counter next to the sink, her arms folded together loosely above her waist.

"You're supposed to be off today, all of you, enjoying yourselves. Why does Emilio have you running errands for him?" Shane asked.

"Neither of you have heard from Emilio in the past hour or so?" Penelope asked. She could feel heat vibrating on her cheeks as she realized she might be in the position to deliver the terrible news.

"No. Who's your friend?" Shane asked.

Penelope introduced Joey, who stepped closer to Penelope

and placed a hand on her shoulder, squeezing gently. "Emilio was taken into custody earlier at the restaurant site. The police have him at the station on the mainland," she said.

"What?" The smile slipped from Dominique's face for the first time since they'd arrived.

Penelope glanced between hers and Shane's expectant faces.

"From what I can tell, they took him in on suspicion of kidnapping. I don't have all of the details. I just happened to be there when it happened, and he asked me to bring these to you."

"What the hell?" Shane yelled, his face going dark red. "Who are they saying he kidnapped?"

"They found my servers, Sabena and Rebekkah, unconscious, padlocked inside the construction site. They've been missing all weekend," Penelope said. "I watched them get wheeled out on stretchers. It was horrible."

"That doesn't mean my Emilio put them there. What proof do they have of anything?" Dominique demanded.

Penelope hesitated a moment then said, "I don't know what proof they have. We were all at the beach party on Friday night, and the police said people saw him talking to the girls after the party had broken up."

A different expression came over Dominique's face. She said harshly, "These girls, how old are they, then?" A slight French accent weaved its way through some of her words.

Penelope pretended to think about her answer before she said, "Sixteen. Both of them."

"*Secousse*," Dominique whispered under her breath, shaking her head.

"Penelope, that's still not solid evidence against Emilio," Shane said in an accusatory tone.

"Who else would have keys to that padlock, Mr. Guthrie?"

Joey said, slipping out of vacation mode and into his homicide detective voice.

"I do, and the foreman on the construction team. And Emilio, of course. The construction crew isn't coming over until tomorrow to set up. I gave the film crew tomorrow off so Emilio and I could spend the day walking the site with the foreman and attending the building planning meeting."

"And you're sure no one else has access to the building?" Joey asked.

"I bought that lock myself. It came with two keys and I had two extra keys made for it. It's in the construction agreement that we allow the city council access, something to do with emergency fire codes because we're not year-round residents. But I haven't given them the key yet. I trust the construction manager and the town manager."

"Trust is an interesting word to use in this situation," Dominique said cryptically. The fine features of her face looked pained, her green eyes welling on the verge of tears. Penelope had never seen a more flawless complexion on a grown woman. Dominique looked like she'd jumped off the pages of a skincare ad in a fashion magazine into this rundown mansion. Judging from her French accent and dark complexion, Penelope guessed she was Creole.

Shane walked to the back wall of the kitchen and cranked open the middle section of the dirty slated windows, his flip flops slapping the tile floor. The windows opened out onto a small deck and an overgrown yard tangled with mangrove and orange trees.

"Did you see Emilio talking with anyone after the party broke up?" Penelope asked.

"Yes," he said, continuing to stare out of the windows. Dominique snorted out a quick harsh laugh.

"When was the last time you heard from Emilio?" Joey asked. Dominique seemed lost in thought, shaking her head slowly back and forth. She didn't appear to have heard what Joey said.

"I spoke to him this morning," Shane said. "He was going to take another look around the site, make sure everything was set for our meeting with the architect and construction workers. They're bringing all of the plans and blueprints for our approval. It's a big day for us."

"Mrs. Babineau," Joey said, turning to Dominique. "You didn't attend the party on Friday night?"

"I wasn't on the island yet. I only came over yesterday. I've been doing the same thing they're doing for the restaurant for the house, meeting with the remodeling team, approving designs and colors, and I had a meeting in the morning before I came. We rent a condo in Miami...I'm really not comfortable sleeping here yet, especially not on my own. If Emilio is here, then sometimes I can rest."

"Where did you guys have lunch yesterday?" Penelope asked.

"The Shrimp Shack on the beach. Why?" Shane said, turning to face them again.

"I was just wondering. Emilio mentioned having lunch with you," Penelope said.

Shane looked confused for a minute, then nodded at Dominique. "We all met at the Shrimp Shack after Dominique arrived on the ferry. Emilio was running behind, but he eventually showed." Dominique nodded in agreement.

Penelope remembered something, then pushed it aside. She placed her hand on Dominique's forearm, the skin cool under her fingers. "I'm sorry to have been the one to tell you this. But Emilio wanted me to come and bring the paperwork to you in person. I hope everything works out. We should get going and let you get in touch with him."

Joey nodded at them and followed Penelope back down the hallway.

"Penelope," Shane called after her.

"Yes?" Penelope said, turning back towards the kitchen.

"Keep this to yourself, okay? I'm sure Emilio has nothing to do with any of this. We don't need any bad press on the set."

CHAPTER 11

Back in the Range Rover, they brushed a few leaves that had fallen through the sunroof off of the tan leather seats.

"Well, that was weird," Joey said. "Did you get the feeling that Babineau's wife wasn't completely surprised he might be involved with young girls?" He started up the truck and backed out of the narrow gravel driveway.

Penelope nodded as she pulled her seatbelt into place. "This isn't the first time he's had problems. He was accused of inappropriate behavior with a couple of students back when I was in school."

Joey cut his eyes at her as he pulled onto the road. "Is Emilio an old flame of yours, Penny? A campus romance from long ago?"

"No," Penelope said sharply, her expression serious. "I heard the rumors about him, and I know he socialized with his students once in a while, but I never believed he acted improperly with the girls back in school. The allegations were dropped. Both of the girls took back what they said, even the one who said they were romantically involved."

"Whatever happened to them?" Joey asked. "Might be interesting to find out, see if there are any similarities."

Penelope nodded, and pulled her phone from her purse.

"I'll Google them, see what comes up. One of the girls involved back then was Summer Farrington. We roomed together first term, but then got shuffled away from each other in the next lottery."

"They made you change roommates every semester?" Joey asked, eyes on the road.

"Yeah, well, after each term, and our school terms were about four months long. The school years are set up differently than regular universities. It's an intensive study, and they think moving people around and having them live and work with different students helps build better chefs."

Penelope tapped a few things on her phone and said, "Here she is. She's chef de cuisine at Saciar in New York."

"The fancy Latin place in Midtown?" Joey asked, sliding his eyes towards her phone.

"Apparently. She looks the same," Penelope said, nodding. She widened a picture on the screen of her phone to look closer at Summer's face.

"She reminds me of you a little," Joey said, taking another quick glance, then pulling his eyes back to the road.

"Yeah, we joked about that our first year, that they roomed us together on purpose because we looked like sisters," Penelope said, remembering. "It was my first time away from home. Everything was so new, and we were under this incredible pressure to succeed or be asked to leave the institute."

"Is Summer the one Emilio was supposedly romantically involved with?" Joey said, his jaw tightening.

"Yeah," Penelope said just above a whisper. "But then later she took back her story, made a deal with Emilio and the school. We weren't roommates anymore when all of that was happening, and she would never talk to anyone about it afterwards, even when Emilio had already left the institute."

"Looks like she turned out okay," Emilio said.

They rode in silence for a few minutes.

"What about the other girl?" Emilio asked. "Can you find anything about her?"

Penelope went back to tapping on her phone. "No...I'm not seeing anything. Her name was Christine Sullivan. Nothing is coming up as far as her working as a chef anywhere that I can find on Google."

"She has a more common name," Joey offered. "Also, she could have gotten married and changed it."

"Maybe. I don't know how I'd find her if that's the case," Penelope said. "Unless..." She pulled open a new search tab on the screen. "The institute has a listing of all students and where they work on their site, not for the public but for fellow students. You can log in and look for classmates, for jobs or referrals, that kind of thing."

"Are you finding her in there?" Joey asked, slowing the truck down to take a turn.

Penelope shook her head. "She's not listed in here, not that I can see. There are a couple of Christines..."

"Jot down their names and do a search; if they have pictures online at the restaurants where they work, you might be able to recognize her."

"Good idea," Penelope said, pulling a pen and paper from her backpack and scribbling down a few names.

"Hey, do you think I caught Dominique and Shane off-guard when I asked about lunch yesterday?" Penelope asked suddenly, looking up from her paper.

"Yeah, I noticed that," Joey said. "Lunch at a public place isn't very hard to confirm, so why would they be cagy about it?"

"Maybe they weren't trying to be evasive, maybe they were just curious why I was asking," Penelope said. "I'm pretty sure

Emilio told me that Shane picked him up at the house for lunch though. Why would he lie about that?"

"Unless he was locking two girls in his construction site before he met them," Joey said darkly.

Penelope paused, unsure of how to feel. She finally said quietly, "Joey, I just know he wouldn't hurt them."

Joey glanced down at the list of names in her lap and then back at the road, staying silent.

After a moment of silence, Penelope said, "It felt weird being the one to tell Dominique that her husband had been arrested."

"You get used to delivering bad news after a while," Joey said quietly.

Penelope laid her hand loosely over his on the center console as they drove back towards town, her eyes flicking from the road to the list of names in her lap.

"Something has me thinking," Penelope said.

Joey slowed down to maneuver a curve in the road up ahead. "What's that?"

"Emilio told the detectives he called his wife Friday night after he got home from the party, but she didn't mention it," Penelope said. "I hope he's not lying about that." Her stomach began to twist, wondering if Emilio was digging himself into a bigger hole by lying to the police.

When they got back on the boat, Penelope and Joey headed to her cabin. Penelope tossed her backpack on the bed and pulled a silver laptop from her overnight bag. "Before we go swimming I'm going to email that detective the employment info on the girls. Go ahead and get changed." They'd decided to stay on the boat with Max and Arlena and swim off the side for the rest of the day. She felt the boat shift beneath her as it powered away from the dock and out to sea.

Joey pulled a pair of swim trunks from his suitcase and stepped into the bathroom, closing the door behind him. Penelope powered up the laptop and logged into the film production website, a shared server that all of the managers on the movie had access to. In her employment folder she located the scanned permissions and electronic time cards for the girls. She found Detective Torres' card in her backpack and emailed her the information with a short note that said, "Attached please find the documents we discussed. Let me know if I can help with anything else."

Penelope bit her bottom lip and opened her browser, typing Rebekkah and Sabena's names into her search engine. A page or so of results filled the screen, linking to the girls' Facebook, Instagram and Twitter accounts.

Joey came out of the bathroom in his trunks holding a bottle of sunscreen. "Can you get some on my back? I can't reach. What are you looking at?"

She waved him over. "I was checking to see if there was any update on the girls. There's nothing about what happened today, but here's an article on Facebook about their school's volleyball team making it to the semifinals." She clicked the link leading to a local news website. A photo of eight girls in volleyball uniforms filled the screen. Sabena and Rebekkah knelt next to each other in the front row, fists on hips.

"Go back to their profiles," Joey said. He sat on the bed behind her and looked at the screen over her shoulder.

Penelope clicked on Sabena's profile first. The profile picture was her sucking in her cheeks and pouting at the camera, long blonde hair framing her face. Her background photo was an artsy shot of a volleyball net. Penelope went into the "About Me" section. "She seems like your average teenager. She likes boy bands, reality shows and the beach. Under 'Relationship' she put 'it's complicated.'"

"Aren't all relationships complicated at that age?" Joey asked.

"It's probably a lot more complicated when you're not allowed to date," Penelope said. She scrolled through Sabena's pictures, not seeing any one particular man more than once, and those were all in group shots.

Penelope clicked on Rebekkah's profile and found much of the same. Her profile picture was a selfie of her and Sabena, their heads pressed together, both of them making the same duck-faced expression. Her background picture was of the ocean, a cameraman from the crew silhouetted against the sunset.

"That's from our set," Penelope said, pointing at the picture. Rebekkah designated herself as single in her settings.

"Click on her pictures," Joey said. "See if either of them posted anything Friday night."

Scanning through the photos, Penelope recognized a few from the party, with piles of crawfish and random groups of people milling around the tables. She saw a picture of herself, Arlena and Gavin sitting at the bar. The caption read, "Hanging with the A-list tonight." Sabena hadn't posted anything from Friday night. Her most recent post from earlier in the week read, "Rough day. Please send prayers." There were several likes and comments below the status update, mostly people responding that they were thinking of her or sending virtual hugs.

"It looks like something was going on with her," Penelope said.

"Maybe," Joey said. "I see posts like that all the time. I

wonder why people are so vague about things going on in their lives when they share everything else."

Penelope stood up from the desk, stretched her arms over her head, then took the suntan lotion from Joey and spread some on his shoulders and back. When she was finished, she pulled a white bikini out of her bag and went into the bathroom to change. When she came out, Joey was sitting at the desk, scrolling through photos. Most of them were of a smiling Sabena either by herself or with other kids who looked to be around her age.

"Find anything else interesting?" she asked.

"Not really, your typical stuff. These kids put everything up online, it's amazing," Joey said, standing up from the desk. "Looks like she has a lot of friends based on how many pictures there are of her with other people."

Penelope grabbed her bag and pulled a pad of paper from it, looking at the different names she'd jotted down. "I'm going to search these Chef Christines. See if anyone looks familiar."

Joey watched over her shoulder as Penelope searched a few names, pulling up the attached images and squinting at each of them.

"These aren't her. This one's way too old," she pointed at the screen, "and the other two don't look like the girl I remember at all."

"It looks like she's not working as a chef anywhere," Joey said.

"I guess not, or at least not in a place where they publicly list their chefs," Penelope said. "She hasn't updated her listing on the institute site either."

"So you think she's working in a chain restaurant or something?" Joey asked.

"You don't need a graduate certificate from the best

culinary school in the country to work in a place like that,"
Penelope said doubtfully. "I wonder what happened to her."

"I'll make a call to the station. One of the guys can do a
search, maybe find out where she ended up," Joey said.

"That would be so helpful," Penelope agreed. "If it's true
and nothing happened with Summer and Christine back in
school, it would make me more confident about believing him
now." Penelope glanced at the screen once more and then slowly
closed the laptop. "Let's go back up."

Max, Arlena, Penelope and Joey spent the afternoon on the
upper deck of the boat, talking and lying in the sun. The captain
had taken them to a remote spot far enough out for some
privacy from Andrea Island but close enough they could still see
the shoreline in the distance.

Max and Arlena had been arguing over whether or not they
should worry about sharks in the water. The argument didn't
last long and soon Joey and Penelope heard splashes and
laughter coming from the ocean three levels down.

"Do you know of anyone who'd want to hurt those girls,
Penny Blue?" Joey asked out of nowhere.

Penelope turned onto her side to face him, propping her
head up. "They're sixteen-year-old girls. How many enemies
could they possibly have?"

"You'd be surprised. Who knows what goes on in the lives
and minds of teenage girls? I've dealt with some seriously mean
girls before. Some of them fight just as much as the boys do,
only their fighting can be even more vicious."

"I never thought about that," Penelope said. "I remember
high school being rough here and there but nothing like that."

"It's easy to overlook when you're so far removed from it,

but bullying has gotten way out of control, especially now with all this online stuff. Kids are ganging up and harassing others through Facebook and Twitter. We don't have any control over it. And the parents...they can't be bothered sometimes." Joey shook his head.

"I suppose the police will be looking into all of that, right?" Penelope asked, sitting up all the way and facing him, cross-legged on her chaise.

"Maybe. Maybe not if they're convinced of Emilio's guilt. It depends on how good the detectives are, what evidence they find."

"So much revolves around technology now. Whenever the girls were on a break they would sit behind the tent and text, or listen to music together. It struck me as funny, because they'd be sitting right next to each other and not talking, but texting on their phones...maybe to each other, who knows?"

"It's a different world." Changing the subject, Joey said, "You ready to go for a swim?"

Penelope gazed out at the ocean, marveling at how it appeared to go on forever until it just dropped off at the edge of the sky. "I'm ready if you are," she said.

CHAPTER 12

Max, Penelope and Joey took a left on Ocean Avenue and headed towards Josie's Shrimp Shack for dinner. Arlena had decided to stay behind on the boat and read, the idea of hanging out at Josie's unappealing to her. The open-air bar looked like it was pieced together with driftwood. Multicolored hurricane lamps made from mason jars hung from wooden beams underneath the thatched roof. Waxy cream-colored candles, nestled in sand from the beach, flickered in more mason jars, illuminating each of the tables.

"You can sit anywhere you like," a woman called to them from across the main room.

They made their way out onto the deck, choosing a square wooden table near the railing in the corner. Penelope gathered her long skirt in her hands before sliding across the bench to her seat, being careful not to pull her long sundress on any splinters.

The same woman who'd greeted them approached their table, tucking a dark curl behind her ear. She wore a black Josie's Shrimp Shack shirt and a short black apron tied tightly at her waist. After they made their drink orders she said, "We have a shrimp feast special tonight, all you can eat for thirty a head. Comes with fries and coleslaw too. If you're interested in our other items, they're listed on the back of the menu. But I highly recommend the shrimp. It's the best deal on the beach tonight. Let me get those beers for you," she said, turning on her white sneakered heel.

The waitress came back with their drinks and they placed their orders, shrimp feasts all around. "Your first batch will be up shortly. My name's Jen. If you need anything just yell or wave me down. I'll be around all night." She moved away quickly to greet new guests at the door.

"She's got a lot of running to do," Penelope said. Most of the seats inside were filled and the patio was filling up too. Besides the bartender Jen seemed to be the only one waiting on customers. Just then a strum of guitar strings sounded over the loud speakers as a man's voice checked the mike.

"Sounds like the band is tuning up," Max said.

Jen returned with their food and drinks, setting everything down quickly in front of them and turning to go.

Max called after her, "Excuse me, who's getting ready to play in there?"

Jen's expression softened. "That's my old man, Jonny, and his friends. He loves getting up there and singing. They do some pretty good classic rock covers." With that she moved away to help a nearby table.

"I'm going to head to the ladies room, excuse me," Penelope said after polishing off a few shrimp. Joey and Max both stood up briefly when she left.

The restaurant's interior was covered in dark wood paneling, a large square bar taking up the majority of the space. A row of tall two-top tables with stools pushed under them lined the back wall. Black and white photos of people in bathing suits lounging on the deck at Josie's hung around the room. Judging from the variety of swimwear and hairstyles, Penelope guessed the photos spanned several decades.

A stage was angled in the front corner, facing out over a scuffed linoleum dance floor. The band was setting up, flinging microphone cords and amp cables around and tuning up their guitars. Penelope popped into the ladies room, then was almost knocked over by Jen as she emerged back into the narrow hallway. Jen apologized and hurried past, pushing her way into the kitchen at the end of the hallway. Catching a glimpse of a familiar young man standing at the counter, Penelope went to the door and pushed it open wide enough to duck her head inside.

"Regan, hey," Penelope said, waving from the doorway.

Regan stood behind a steel table in the middle of the kitchen, picking through a pile of shrimp.

Regan looked up with a surprised smile. "What're you doing here, Boss?"

"Having dinner with some friends," Penelope said, stepping all the way into the kitchen.

Jen was busy at the back counter, pulling shrimp from the steamer, dusting them with seasoning and filling up clean baskets for service. She had a cordless phone wedged between her ear and shoulder as she worked. "We close at two a.m....Yes, there's live music tonight...Okay, no, no reservations, just come on down...Okay, see you then." She pulled off her plastic glove and ended the call, hanging the phone back in its cradle on the wall. When she saw Penelope in the kitchen she froze and said, "Did you need something, hon?"

Regan introduced Jen to Penelope, who turned out to be his mother.

"Oh, it's nice to meet you. Regan just loves working on that set." She excused herself as the phone rang again, grabbing it and a tray of shrimp before pushing her way back out the kitchen door.

"Regan, can I ask you something?" Penelope said after she'd gone. She watched him sort through the shrimp and saw he was quick and efficient about it.

"Sure," Regan said, pausing for a minute and looking at up her.

"Did you hear what happened to Rebekkah and Sabena?"

"Yeah, I did," Regan said, looking back down at the shrimp and resuming his sorting. His shoulders stiffened under his Josie's t-shirt. "I had to talk to the police today. This lady cop came in here and asked me a bunch of questions."

"Detective Torres?"

"Yeah, that's her," Regan said.

"Were you with Rebekkah and Sabena on Friday night? Francis said you offered to get them home safely. Did something happen?" Penelope kept her tone neutral, worried she might scare him into silence.

"Yes," Regan said after a moment. "That crawfish guy with the French name? He came over and started talking to us. Like talking to all of us, but mostly talking to Sabena. He said he had no way to get home and that he'd give us beer if I gave him a ride." Regan looked down at the shrimp in front of him as he spoke.

Penelope's heart sank and she took a breath. "What happened after that? Did you drive him home?"

"Yeah, I did," Regan said quietly.

"And the girls? Did you give them a ride too?" Penelope prodded. Outside, the band had started playing their version of the old Beach Boys song "I Get Around."

"That's the part that I feel really bad about, but, yeah, they came along for the ride to that dude's house. He was pretty drunk and kept trying to give me a beer while I was driving. I can't do anything like that. My parents are cool about me having a drink or two, but they'd flip out and take my car away if I got caught drinking and driving."

Penelope nodded. "Were Rebekkah and Sabena drinking?"

Regan nodded and leaned against the counter behind him. He pulled his plastic gloves off and folded his arms at his chest. "That's the messed-up part," he said. "I was hanging out with them before we left and they seemed fine, just drinking water. And then suddenly they're wasted. Rebekkah said something like 'that vodka we drank,' and I got the feeling they'd spiked their water bottles. Sabena said she swiped some pharms from her mom too."

"Pharms?" Penelope said.

"Yeah, you know. Pills," Regan said. "Swiping a pill or two from your parents' medicine cabinet is the safest way to catch a buzz. They never miss them."

Penelope paused as the kitchen door swung open again. Jen rushed in. "We just sat three new tables. We got enough picked through for a few hours?"

"Yeah, Mom," Regan said.

"Good. Hey, go listen to your dad play for a while. Put that shrimp in the walk-in and take a break. I'll let you know if I need you again. Go have some fun." She squeezed him on the arm and went back out the door.

"Did you end up taking the girls home after you dropped Emilio at his house?" Penelope asked when they were alone again.

"No," Regan said, shaking his head. "They shared a beer in the car on the way out there, but when we got to the other side of the island I had to pull over because Sabena got sick. She was really upset, thought she was going to get into trouble with her mom for being drunk. I get the feeling she isn't a very experienced partier. She was upset about something...something about her boyfriend. Honestly they were drunk so I tried to tune them out. I offered to take them somewhere else, but they just both kept saying that they were going to get killed when they got home."

Penelope closed her eyes. "What happened after that?"

"I didn't want to leave them with that guy, but he said he knew you, like, for a long time. He was your teacher or something? And that his wife was cool with the girls coming in and sobering up for a while. He said Rebekkah and Sabena could stay at his place until they all felt better and then he would drive them home. I saw a big white pickup truck parked at the house. He said they only needed an hour or two and some water. Rebekkah said they'd text their moms saying they were staying at each other's houses for the night, and then they'd slip back into her bedroom after her parents fell asleep."

Penelope felt sick to her stomach and put a hand on the steel table, focusing on the cool metal.

"So the last time you saw them they were at Emilio's house?"

"Well, they were heading inside. I watched him unlock the door, to make sure they weren't locked out, and then I took off."

"They didn't invite you in?" Penelope asked.

"They did, but I had to get home. And I'd had enough teenage drama at that point," Regan said.

"Did you tell all of that to Detective Torres?"

"Yeah. She made a call after that and left in a hurry," Regan said. "I didn't want to rat anybody out, but I didn't want them thinking I was messing around with those girls either. I'm an adult now. Messing around with a sixteen-year-old, even if she's your girlfriend, can get you in serious trouble."

"Regan, do you remember seeing me early on Saturday morning up on the avenue?" Penelope asked.

"When...Saturday morning?" Regan said, a blush coming to his cheeks.

"Yes, around seven thirty I found you passed out outside of Rose's. I helped you onto the park bench, but then you were gone when I came back out to check on you."

"Oh, that. Yeah, I did end up partying a little bit more on my own after I got back. But I didn't drive," Regan said, regaining some of his composure. "I went to Aunt Rose's for a pack of cigarettes, and I guess I fell asleep."

"Rose is your aunt?" Penelope asked.

"No, but she's practically family. My dad's parents passed away when he was young. She and my grandma were close, and she stepped in to help out with stuff for him, school and whatnot. We spend the holidays with her, you know, family stuff. I help her out with the rental cabins too, cleaning them out when people leave or helping show them to new renters."

"Regan," Penelope said. "You're an adult and I'm not trying to make you feel like you're not, but you know it isn't safe to drink until you pass out, right?"

"I'm really embarrassed that you saw me that way," Regan said, picking up a dishtowel and twisting it around his fist. "That was one night when I just let myself go. But I don't do that all the time. You can trust me. I hope you still want me to work for you."

Penelope sighed. "I think you have real potential. I'm just worried about you. You have to take better care of yourself. But yeah, I'd like to see you at work on Tuesday."

"Thanks, Miss Sutherland, I promise I won't act like a fool again."

"Good," Penelope said. The band started playing "Good Lovin'" to a round of cheers from the bar patrons. "I should get back to my friends. Are you coming out?"

"Yeah, I'm right behind you," he said, pulling off his apron.

They walked out to the bar area together. Regan leaned down and shouted over the music, pointing at the lead singer. "That's my dad, Jonny. He's the front man and the other guys are his two best friends."

Jonny gripped his microphone with both hands, holding it close to his lips. He was tall and slim with shoulder-length black hair that whipped around as he sang. A full-grown version of Regan, he looked to be in his mid-forties.

"You look a lot like your dad," Penelope shouted over the music.

Regan pointed to a picture over the bar. It was a large black and white photograph of a woman sitting on the beach in a one-piece bathing suit, smiling serenely, a chubby baby waving from her lap. Judging from her hair and sunglasses, Penelope guessed the picture was from the late sixties or early seventies. "That's my grandmother, Josie Daniels. People say I look a lot like her. That's my dad when he was a baby. Josie opened up the Shrimp Shack right before that picture was taken, but passed away soon after that. We carry it on in her name. Keep the tradition of shrimp on the beach." Someone at the bar caught Regan's attention and Penelope followed his gaze. Max and Gavin were sitting together at the bar, laughing about something.

"Max just arrived on the island the other day," Penelope shouted over the music.

"He's in the movie?" Regan asked, taking another look. "I've seen his reality show."

"Yep. Arlena always tries to get him parts in her projects."

"I'm going out for a smoke," Regan said, stepping away from her and heading to the patio. He pulled a silver cigarette box from his pocket with a distinctive holographic on the side that glinted in the dim lights.

"Where did you get those?" Penelope asked, following him outside.

"Rose's," Regan said. "She's the only one who sells smokes on the island."

"You should think about quitting," Penelope said, trying to sound like a friend and not a preachy adult.

Regan smiled and shrugged. "I will."

Penelope returned to her table, where Joey sat alone.

"I thought you ditched me," Joey said. He looked content. The relaxed atmosphere of the beach seemed to be agreeing with him.

"No way," Penelope said, glancing at Regan smoking at the far end of the patio. "I was talking with one of my helpers. Joey, Emilio was with those girls Friday night at his house. Regan drove them all there after the party."

"That doesn't sound good, Penny," Joey said, his relaxed expression hardening.

"I know," Penelope said. "I'm at a loss as to how to feel."

Joey grabbed her hand and squeezed her fingers between his. Penelope fell silent and stared towards the bar, just as the band finished another song. Jen stepped up on the stage and sang a soulful version of "Gold Dust Woman," the room falling silent except for her voice.

"You ready to go?" Joey asked, after the song was finished.

Penelope realized she had been quiet for a while, going over everything she had learned about Emilio in her mind, trying to fit all of the different stories together.

"Yeah, let's go," Penelope said. She slid out from the booth and waved goodbye to Regan on the way out.

CHAPTER 13

The next morning, Penelope and Joey decided to have breakfast at the Inn and then pick up his cabin rental keys from Rose afterwards.

"Good morning, Penelope," Jeanne said as she greeted them at the hostess podium.

Penelope introduced Joey to Jeanne who then led them to a table near the window. She wore pale green Capri pants and a matching short jacket with a white t-shirt underneath. Penelope thought she always managed to look professional and comfortable at the same time. "We haven't had this many new people on Andrea Island for as long as I can remember," Jeanne said as she handed them their menus. "And that's a long time. Coffee for you both?"

They nodded and she hurried away, returning with a carafe a few minutes later. Joey and Penelope made their breakfast orders and sat drinking their coffee and watching the water. The dining room was about half-full, Penelope recognizing all of the other diners as members of the film crew.

"This is the only hotel on the island?" Joey asked, looking up at the ceiling.

Penelope nodded. "Jeanne took it over from her parents,

and they did from her grandparents. She grew up here and now she's in charge."

Jeanne came over with their plates of eggs, bacon and hash browns. "You all should come to the Happiest Hour tonight. Have a cocktail with us before dinner."

Jeanne threw a cocktail party every evening on the rooftop deck of the Inn for both her guests and friends on the island. Penelope had attended a few, along with most of the rest of the cast and crew.

"Maybe we will," Penelope said. "Joey's going to get settled into his cabin today, but I'm sure we'll want to get out later."

"Are you with the film crew?" Jeanne asked.

"No, ma'am," Joey said, setting down his coffee mug. "I'm just visiting Penny for a few days."

"What do you do for work back home?" Jeanne asked.

"I work for the city," Joey said, glancing away from her.

"He's a homicide detective," Penelope said, lowering her voice. Joey didn't always feel comfortable announcing that he was a detective, especially when he was off duty.

Jeanne raised a hand to her heart. "My stars, a homicide detective?" Jeanne's cheerful smile faltered a bit, then she recovered.

"Yes, ma'am. New Jersey PD," Joey said, giving her a quick smile.

"Welcome to our island," Jeanne said, shifting back into hospitality mode. "We're getting all kinds of folks around here lately."

"Jeanne, have you heard any updates about Sabena and Rebekkah? Do you know how they're doing?" Penelope said.

Jeanne's expression became grave and she lowered her voice. "From what I heard, both girls overdosed on something and they haven't woken up yet. Sabena had a seizure and now she's on life support, and they're not sure if she's going to make it through, poor little thing. It's really terrible, Penelope."

Penelope's heart sank. "How terrible."

"Yes, it is. Between you and me, I don't understand why young people today get into drugs. When we were that age no one told us anything, we had to figure it all out for ourselves. But there's so much information available now. I just hate thinking about the state they're in."

They all sat in silence for a moment, unsure of where to take the conversation from there.

"Even after all of this ugliness, I still hope you enjoy your vacation," Jeanne said, attempting to lighten the mood. "Enjoy your breakfast and let me know if I can get anything else for you."

Jeanne began to turn away from the table and Penelope said, "Jeanne, can I ask you a favor?"

"Of course, dear," Jeanne said, her smile reappearing.

"I want to have a quick meeting with my chefs a little later. Can I use your library for fifteen minutes or so?"

"Yes, that would be fine. Just poke your head in and let me know and I'll remember not to go in and disturb you."

"Thanks, Jeanne."

After breakfast Joey and Penelope walked hand in hand down the sidewalk to Rose's. The door was propped open with a large piece of coral and they entered, their eyes adjusting to the dark interior from the bright morning sun. Rose was sitting on a stool behind the counter, a mug of coffee in one hand and a paperback in the other.

"Good morning, Penelope," she said, looking up from her book.

"Hi, Rose. This is my friend Joseph Baglioni. He rented a cabin and needs to pick up the keys."

"Sure, I'll just need a picture ID and a credit card," Rose said. She set down her coffee mug and placed her book facedown on the counter.

Joey pulled his wallet from his back pocket and flipped it open to retrieve his driver's license and credit card. His New Jersey police identification was visible behind the plastic of the flap. Rose glanced at it. "You're a detective? Are you here about those poor girls?"

Joey handed Rose his cards and flipped his wallet closed. "Yes, I'm a detective, but no, I'm not here on a case, just vacation."

"I see. Well, I think you're the first police detective we've had staying on our beach." She wrote down his license number and credit card information in her binder and had him sign on the line next to his entry. She grabbed a set of keys from the wooden cabinet. "You're in number thirteen, the blue one farthest down the beach. My phone number is on the key ring if you need anything once you're there. I've got you booked until Saturday, but if anything changes just let me know. Your card will be charged when you check out."

"I'm looking forward to relaxing on the beach," Joey said.

"I sure do hope you enjoy your stay."

"Rose, have you heard any news about Rebekkah and Sabena?" Penelope asked.

"No," Rose said, shaking her head quickly. "Saw all the commotion over there though. They arrested that big-shot chef right outside on the sidewalk after they found them inside."

"Yeah, I saw that too," Penelope said.

"Well, it's good they got him off the streets, if he's that kind of person," Rose said, pursing her lips.

"Do you know the girls well?" Penelope asked.

Rose shrugged her shoulders in a quick snap. "A little. I know everyone around here. I can't think of either of them ever getting into trouble before. But then again, it only takes one time to make a big mistake."

"I guess," Penelope said.

"It's the truth, dear. Kids make stupid decisions, end up in the path of the wrong person...I feel real bad for the parents."

Penelope nodded and studied the wooden cigarette display case behind the counter. She didn't see any of the silver cigarette packs mixed in with the other brands on the wall.

"Do you carry imported cigarettes?" Penelope asked.

Rose looked behind her at the display case. "No, just the usual American brands. That English actor, Gary? He was asking me the same thing. I told him to try American Spirit if he wanted something different."

"Gavin," Penelope said.

"Huh?" Rose said.

"His name's Gavin."

"Right, Gavin. Well, Gary, Gavin, whatever his name is...I can't bring in L&Bs for him. I don't have the license." She reached down, patted the cigarette pack in her pocket and stepped around the counter.

"Have you decided to start smoking, Penny Blue?" Joey asked.

"No," Penelope said, sighing. "Let's go see your cabin."

Penelope suggested they check out the cabin first, make a trip to Sackler's to pick up anything Joey might need and then swing back by the boat to get his suitcase. They walked past Josie's, heading for the blue cabin about a half-mile down the beach.

Penelope loved all of the multicolored cabins that dotted the shore. They were all unique, differing slightly in style and shape. But they were all in good condition, considering they were older buildings. Joey's was set up much like the cabins her fellow crew members were staying in. It had a spacious sitting room, a small kitchen with white countertops and appliances off to the right and two bedrooms and a bath down a small hallway to the left.

"This is perfect," Joey said. "I'm going to give up my apartment and move in here permanently."

Penelope laughed. "Joey Baglioni, professional beach bum. I can see that." Penelope's phone buzzed in her backpack and she pulled it off of her shoulders to take the call. She glanced at the screen before answering. "Hey, Francis."

"Hey, Boss," he said. "Everyone's back. The guys were on the morning ferry. You still want to get together with us today?"

"Yes, let's all meet at the Inn's library at noon. Let the guys know, okay?"

"Sure. See you then," Francis said.

Penelope hung up. "Ready to get some groceries?"

"What do you want for dinner, Penny?" Joey asked as they wandered through the aisles of Sackler's Market. He stopped suddenly. "I mean, would you like to have dinner with me tonight? I'd love to cook for you."

Penelope laughed. "Yes, I would, thank you."

Joey chuckled. "Sorry, I just assumed we'd have dinner together, but then I realized you could already have plans."

"No, I just have my meeting and then I'm free. I want to spend as much time with you as I can while you're here."

Henny helped Joey pick out some chicken breasts and

steaks in the back case. "So, this is the New Jersey police detective I've been hearing about today," Henny said when Penelope introduced him.

"You've heard about me?" Joey asked with a cautious smile.

"Sure. Jeanne said you had breakfast this morning with Penelope up at the Inn," she said.

"That was an hour ago," Joey said. "You must be on a news hotline."

"Well, me and Jeanne, we talk every day, sometimes a couple times a day. She keeps tabs on the north end, and I keep her posted on the south end of the beach," Henny said in a matter-of-fact tone.

Joey thanked her and picked out some additional groceries in the pantry area. By the time he headed to the register his arm was straining under the weight of the basket. He held a case of Corona in his other hand.

"You have to get all of that back down the beach, you know," Penelope teased him. She started placing his purchases on the frayed conveyer belt that led up to the register manned by Henny's son.

"I'll make it," Joey said. "It looks like more than it really is."

When it was their turn at the register, Penelope said hi to Bradley.

"Hey, Miss Sutherland," he said, scanning through their groceries and placing them into paper bags at Joey's request.

"Your mom's got you working today, huh?" Penelope asked.

"Yeah. It's been busy too," he said, sighing. "She's going to have to find someone to replace me in the fall. I'm off to school in Texas."

"That's great, congratulations," Penelope said. "What are you going to study?"

Bradley continued to scan the items across the foggy

scanner screen, stopping occasionally to punch in numbers on the register. "I'm not sure. Business maybe. I'm going to play baseball. I'm hoping to play professionally after school. I got a full scholarship." He spoke quietly and focused on the groceries, not looking at her.

"Wow, Bradley. That's really something," Penelope said. "An out-of-state school can be so expensive; that's got to be a big relief for your mom."

Bradley nodded quietly and gave her a quick smile, then went back to focus on his work.

Penelope decided she would never understand teenagers. Bradley didn't seem very excited about his scholarship. If Penelope had gotten a full-ride to culinary school at his age, she would've been bouncing off the walls with excitement. "Are you looking forward to school?"

"Yeah," he said, scanning the last item and looking up at her. He seemed on the verge of saying something else, then paused and said, "I'm glad I got the scholarship. It's my ticket out. We probably couldn't have swung the tuition ourselves. When my dad got sick...well, there wasn't much left in the savings when he died."

"I'm so glad that worked out for you. Are you worried about leaving home?" Penelope asked.

He looked at her and thought for a moment. "No," he said finally.

Joey and Penelope headed down the sidewalk back towards the cabin, loaded down with groceries.

"That kid looked familiar," Joey said. "I'm pretty sure I saw him in a couple of the Facebook photos we were looking at earlier."

"Yeah? It's got to be a small school. He plays baseball and the girls play volleyball. I'm sure they all know each other."

Joey was quiet for a moment then said, "Why don't you go on ahead to your meeting? I'll get everything back to the cabin and get set up." He motioned for her to give him the shopping bag she was carrying.

"Are you sure?" Penelope asked, reluctantly handing it over.

"Yeah, I'll pick up my suitcase too, get settled. And then I'm going to camp out on one of those deck chairs outside of my temporary home with a book."

"Okay, I'll see you later," Penelope said, kissing him on the cheek before turning to head back to the Inn. She greeted a few crew members she passed on her way and thought about Bradley and his scholarship. Then she thought about Regan, who might just be stuck there, anchored by a family business. She tried to put herself in their shoes, just out of high school, trying to find their way. Andrea Island was a paradise for vacationers, hikers and fishermen, but she didn't imagine there was much opportunity for the younger generation to explore new things. Some of the established residents of the island were so resistant to outsiders and change, getting approval and all of the necessary permits needed to film for three months had delayed the start of production two months longer than any other movie she'd worked on.

As she passed by the path that led to the marina, she saw the *Isn't She Lovely* bobbing up and down in its slip and heard the midday ferry horn sound as it pulled away from the dock. The flash of a Hawaiian shirt and spiky black hair caught her eye. She stopped short to pull her sunglasses down, took another look and saw Emilio Babineau walking towards her.

CHAPTER 14

When Emilio met up with Penelope at the end of the path, his expression changed from anxiousness to relief.

"Chef," Penelope said. "What are you doing here?"

"I made bail this morning. Had to wait until Monday for the court to be in session. Don't get arrested over the weekend if you can help it," he said, grimacing. "I've got a meeting with Shane and the developers in a few. I've got to get to the house to shower and change."

"What's happening with your case?" Penelope asked.

Emilio shrugged. "I don't know. I have good lawyers on my side. They're not going to get me on this, Penelope. I haven't done anything illegal."

"I know the girls were with you on Friday night, Chef," Penelope said. "Regan told me all three of you went into your house after he dropped you off. Did you tell the police the truth about that?" She folded her arms across her chest and took a step back from him.

Emilio squinted at her behind his sunglasses. He smelled like sweat and his face was shiny under his spiky black hair. "Yeah, that's what he told the cops. But then he drove away. Those girls came inside for a few minutes to sober up. They were going to get in trouble with their parents for being wasted. I went upstairs to call Dominique, and when I came back down they'd taken off."

"You lied to me," Penelope said, color coming into her cheeks. "I never wanted to believe the rumors about you back in school, you know, the ones about you messing around with your students? You never acted that way around me, and I defended you when everyone was talking about what happened with Christine and Summer behind your back. Looks like I was a fool."

"Penelope, Summer lied about what happened between us. We were never romantically involved," Emilio said.

Penelope looked at him skeptically, trying to contain the anger that was bubbling to the surface. "Then why did she say you two slept together? That's what she said, isn't it? That's why you left school in the middle of the term...you couldn't keep your hands off of her?"

"Penelope, don't say that. You know she took the story back, that we all signed an agreement," Emilio said, his voice hardening.

Penelope sighed. "What was in the agreement you signed?"

"Both girls recanted their stories to the dean, and I agreed to sever ties with the institute," Emilio said quietly.

"But if you didn't do anything wrong, why leave? If they lied, then..." Penelope said, trying to fit the pieces together.

"They were students, so the benefit of the doubt fell in their favor. Nothing could be proven, because nothing happened," Emilio added quickly, "but it was a disruption that the administration didn't appreciate. Then some of the parents raised concerns about me. Sometimes the appearance of impropriety is just as bad. In the end, it was agreed I should leave, and I took a severance settlement and went. Opened Craw Daddy's with it."

Penelope thought again to her days at culinary school, about how young she was, roughly the same age as both Summer and Christine. The memories of their faces began to mix with the slightly younger ones of Rebekkah and Sabena, and she felt a sense of helplessness come over her.

"You were right to defend me back then," Emilio said, "And I'm sorry I disappointed you. I've had some problems in my past, but I've remade myself. I'm happy, I love my wife. She's the only woman I ever want or need."

Penelope wished she could see his eyes behind his dark lenses.

"And I didn't lie to you about Friday night, I just knew how the truth would sound, so I just didn't tell you everything that happened," Emilio said in a soothing tone. "I need someone on my side in this."

"Not telling me the whole story and asking me to help you is the same thing as lying," Penelope said. "I don't know how to feel about you anymore. It's like the whole thing that happened with Christine and Summer is happening all over again. And here I am again, being put in the position to defend you."

"Penelope, believe me, please," Emilio said, scuffing the toe of his boot on the sidewalk. "I've always been good to you, helped you whenever I could. We worked closely together back in school all the time...did you ever feel threatened by me or feel like I was being inappropriate?"

Penelope looked out over the water, not responding. She filed through her memory, thinking of all the times they'd been alone in the kitchen, him leaning over her to demonstrate the perfect technique. She had to admit, she'd never felt an inappropriate vibe from him, but she also struggled with separating those feelings from the various accusations she'd heard.

"Thanks for getting that paperwork to Dominique," Emilio said, interrupting her thoughts.

Penelope said flatly, "I didn't love being the one to tell her and Shane about you being arrested."

"Shane?" Emilio asked.

"I went over there right after you got...right after it happened. Shane was at your house, so I told them both at the same time."

Emilio paused for a beat then smiled widely. "I see. Sorry about that too, but I appreciate that he heard it from you than from someone else."

"Shane also said you were running late for lunch on Saturday. I thought you said he picked you up," Penelope said in an accusatory tone. She was having a hard time looking directly at him, and continued to gaze at the ocean.

"He did pick me up, but I had him drop me at the city council building for a meeting first. It ran long because the town manager had more papers for me to file," Emilio said evenly. "You been checking up on me?"

Penelope unfolded her arms and shrugged, pulling her gaze to his sunglasses. "I have no idea what to think or feel. And you just said you keep things to yourself when they make you look bad. Why should I believe you now? None of this makes sense and those girls—"

"Which girls are you talking about now, Penelope?" Emilio asked. "From now or from then?"

"You know what? I have to go. Good luck with everything."

Emilio smiled weakly at her, then turned and walked away. Penelope pulled her phone from her backpack and called Joey, leaving him a message. "Hey, it's me. Can you do me a favor? I need some more information on Emilio Babineau."

She clicked off and scrolled to a new screen on her phone,

tapping a phone number to call. The phone rang a few times on the other end and then someone answered, "Saciar."

"Hello, can I speak with Summer Farrington?" Penelope asked.

"Chef's not in the restaurant right now, can I take a message?" the young man asked. Penelope could hear the distinct sounds of an industrial kitchen in the background, pots clanging and several voices shouting over each other.

"Yes, please tell her Penelope Sutherland called. Let me give you my number."

CHAPTER 15

Penelope's staff sat in the stuffed leather chairs of the Inn's library, a sunny room with built-in bookshelves full of novels, nonfiction books and travel guides. Jeanne let anyone on the island borrow books as long as they didn't abuse the privilege. There was only one shelf in the very top corner that no one could borrow from that held a few leather-bound books that looked as old as the Inn itself. A large photograph of a much younger Jeanne and her late husband hung on the wall between the windows. They were toasting with wine glasses on the deck of a boat, beaming widely at the camera.

"I'm glad we're all back together," Penelope said, laying her backpack down on the round oak card table and taking a seat at one of the matching chairs.

Quentin and Francis hid smiles under their hands as they looked at their exhausted coworkers.

"You guys okay?" Penelope asked.

One of her assistant chefs leaned forward and took a deep breath. "Yes, ma'am, we're just a little tired is all."

"Looks more like you're hungover," Penelope said sternly. "Look, I won't keep you long. Do whatever you want today, but I need you all coming to work fresh in the morning. I suggest water and Advil. And sleep."

"No problem," Francis said, and the others nodded.

"I also wanted to fill you in on what happened after the party on Friday, since it involves members of our crew." Penelope let them know most of what had occurred over the weekend, watching their expressions morph from surprise to concern. After answering a few questions of their questions, she went over proposed menus for the upcoming week and gave them their prep assignments. "We're expecting a delivery too, so...you," she said, choosing the chef who looked slightly worse for wear from his weekend, "meet the midday ferry and transport everything back to the tent. Borrow a truck from transportation."

"Sure thing, Boss," he said.

"Okay, you guys take it easy and I'll see you all in the morning. Call time is seven so everyone be in the tent by five."

Penelope stood up and grabbed her backpack, leaving her team to work out the details of their assignments together. Inside the dining room, Penelope spotted Gavin, Arlena and Max with a woman she didn't recognize. She walked over to say hello.

"Pen! That was fun last night, right?" Max asked.

"Sure," Penelope said with less enthusiasm.

Gavin stood up. "Penelope, this is my fiancée, Sienna Wentworth."

"Of course, I heard you were coming to visit."

"She just got here on the midday," Arlena said. "We're going back to the boat to talk concepts and have Sienna take the measurements for my dress." Sienna was an up-and-coming British designer that Arlena had been looking forward to collaborating with on some new looks.

Sienna smiled and took a sip of her iced tea. "Lovely to be here. The weather's gorgeous." In contrast to Gavin, who came off more like a rugby player, Sienna's English accent was light and airy, and she had an elegant way about her.

"I'll be by the boat later to get my things. Joey just checked into his cabin, so I'll either stay over with him or be in my room upstairs."

"There's no rush, whenever you want is fine. I asked Sam if he wouldn't mind keeping the boat docked here for a few weeks. I prefer staying on it."

Penelope wished them luck with their fitting and excused herself. She went upstairs, unlocked the door of her room and went inside, closing it softly behind her. Deciding to take a few minutes to savor the relative peace and quiet, she slid onto the bed, the springs squeaking gently beneath her, and laid her head on the pillow. She closed her eyes, turned onto her side away from the window and drifted off to sleep.

Penelope woke feeling like she'd been asleep for days rather than hours. The sun was much lower in the sky than it was when she'd first curled up. She glanced at the digital clock on the nightstand and saw that it was almost three, which meant she had napped for over two hours. Getting up to stretch, she walked towards the window, opened the thin French doors and stepped out onto the small balcony, yawning and rubbing the sleep from her eyes. The breeze was warm in the lazy afternoon sun. She gazed out at the ocean, noticing a scattering of beach umbrellas and chairs on the sand and a few people out swimming, their heads bobbing up and down in the surf.

Penelope looked over the railing at the pool below. Two of her chefs were asleep on the shady side of the patio, sprawled across two of the chaise lounges. To the left of the pool area she saw Gavin leaning up against the wooden railing in the patio dining area smoking a cigarette. Penelope pulled in a few deep breaths and looked back at the water, watching a couple floating together on a large raft. A flash of black in the corner of her eye brought her attention back to the deck. Regan had appeared next to Gavin, smoking alongside him. She eyed them curiously, observing their body language. Regan seemed agitated and Gavin sympathetic, soothing Regan but shaking his head no. Then Regan hugged Gavin, knotting his hands loosely around the other man's shoulders while Gavin patted him firmly on the back, his cigarette tucked tightly between two fingers. After a few moments Regan pulled away, nodded and left. Gavin watched Regan walk away and continued to smoke, finally turning to look out over the ocean, leaning his forearms on the railing.

Her phone pinged inside her room, and Penelope stepped back inside. She pulled a bottle of water from the mini fridge that hummed in the corner of the room and her phone from her backpack. She went back out onto the balcony and sat down in one of the metal patio chairs, propping her elbow on the matching table. She sipped her water and glanced at the screen, seeing that a few text messages had come in during her nap. There was a group text sent to the movie department heads from the production office confirming their start time in the morning, and another from Francis reminding her of a few items they needed to add to their next food order. Max texted to see if she would like to join him and Arlena at the Happiest Hour up on the roof of the Inn, and the last one from Joey simply read, "How you doing, beautiful?"

Penelope smiled and swiped her phone open to call him.

"There you are," Joey said, sounding relaxed.

"Hey. I came up to my room after my meeting and fell asleep," Penelope said. "What have you been up to?"

"I went swimming in the ocean right outside of my cabin. Then I read for a while out here on my deck. You know, vacation stuff. What's up this evening?"

"I was wondering if you'd like to come to the Inn for happy hour. Jeanne puts on a nice little spread and Max and Arlena will be there. Then we can go back and have dinner at your place, unless you've changed your mind about cooking," Penelope said.

"Perfect," Joey said. "I'll get cleaned up and meet you over there."

"It's from four to six, so come whenever you're ready," she said.

As Penelope stepped out of the shower a few minutes later, she heard her phone ringing in the other room. She pulled a towel around herself and hurried to answer it, grabbing it from the table next to the windows. "Hello?" she said breathlessly.

"Penelope Sutherland?" a woman's voice asked.

"Yes," Penelope answered, pulling the corner of the towel up to dab her face.

"It's Summer Farrington. I got your message…"

"Summer, thanks for calling me back," Penelope said. She glanced behind her at her wet footprints on the carpet leading back to the bathroom.

"Good to hear from you after all this time. I looked you up on the registry. You're based in Jersey?" Summer asked. She sounded like she was outside, definitely away from her loud kitchen.

"Yes, I didn't get too far away from home. Or school," Penelope said.

"Great, well, if you want to send in your resume, I think I can get you a job at the restaurant," Summer said cheerfully. "I don't have anything full-time, but if you—"

"Oh, no, that's not why I called," Penelope interrupted.

"I just assumed that's why I was hearing from you after all this time," Summer said, laughing lightly. "I didn't see your current position listed online."

"No, it's nothing like that. Actually, I called because...remember Emilio Babineau?" Penelope ventured, her body tensing beneath her towel.

"Emilio, how could I forget?" Summer said, her tone losing its cheerful tone. "You're calling me after all these years about him?"

"Yes, I just wanted to know...what actually happened between you two, Summer?" Penelope asked.

Summer blew out a sigh, then laughed quickly. "I can't say. I signed an agreement with the school. Nobody talks, everything goes away. The precious reputation of the institute is saved."

"I'm not the press. I'm not asking you in an official way. I just need to know for myself," Penelope said, sitting down in one of the chairs and bunching the towel tighter around her chest.

"Did he try something on you back then too?" Summer asked, her voice hard, determined.

"I can't really say, but..." Penelope paused, making up a story in her head. "I ran into him again recently, and I've been thinking about everything that happened at school, with you and Christine. You and I were close before, we were all in the same track together, working with him all the time. I've never thought to tell anyone before now, but I know you—"

"Right. Who wines and dines their students? Impressionable young girls away from home? Him with his smooth talk and swagger. Such a pig," Summer said spitefully.

"So, what actually happened between you two?" Penelope asked again, prodding her. "It was all after we were living together, and we've never talked about it."

"I'm sure what happened to me is the same thing that happened to you," Summer said crisply. "I bet our stories are very similar. We should compare notes, then you can get whatever information you need."

"Did you two really sleep together, back in school?" Penelope ventured, tightening her grip on the phone in her hand. Her heart was skipping in her chest and she felt a bit faint. She always had a hard time lying but hoped her voice didn't betray that right now.

"Yes," Summer said without hesitation.

"Can you prove it?" Penelope said, closing her eyes. "Did you ever tell anyone about it?"

"No, and I can't say it anywhere officially either, or I lose my settlement. And any leverage I have left over the jerk," Summer said. "But I'll back your story, as long as I don't violate the terms of my agreement."

"What about Christine? Didn't she know about you and Emilio too?" Penelope asked.

"I don't know. She had a different kind of complaint against him," Summer said quickly. "She wouldn't back my story up completely when I asked her to, but I know he messed around with her too. She was just too afraid to speak up. I'm the one that made her go to the dean."

"What happened to Christine? I didn't see her in the school directory, and she doesn't show up as working anywhere that I can find," Penelope said, her shoulders caving under the weight of the conversation.

"I don't know. Last I heard she was moving north, Vermont maybe. Between you and me, she didn't have the mettle to cut it in this business. She's sweet, but that doesn't get you very far, especially if you want to be taken seriously in a male-dominated kitchen."

Penelope thought for a beat then said, "Can I call you again, after I get my mind around what happened with all of this?"

"Sure, this is my cell. Call me direct. And if you ever want that job..."

"Thanks, Summer," Penelope said, hanging up.

CHAPTER 16

Penelope slipped into a dark red sundress and twisted her long blonde hair into a loose bun at the nape of her neck. When she got downstairs she glanced into the library and saw Jeanne slowly gathering up the scattered sections of a newspaper and straightening the club chairs around the game tables. She was turned away from the door and dressed for her cocktail party in a pretty floral tea-length dress, the skirt swaying around her shins as she moved through the room.

"Hi, Jeanne," Penelope said.

"My stars, Penelope, you gave me a fright," Jeanne said, jumping a little, then quickly wiping a tear from her cheek.

"I'm sorry," Penelope said, taking another step into the room. "I didn't mean to startle you. I just wanted to thank you for letting me use the library earlier. Are you okay?"

Jeanne laughed nervously. "I'm just being silly. Sorry, dear." She swiped more tears from her cheeks. "I'm going to have to touch up my makeup."

"Is something wrong?" Penelope asked.

Jeanne shook her head, her hair waving softly around her pretty face, her glasses swinging by the lanyard around her neck. "I just...I don't know. I guess I get a little sentimental sometimes." She motioned towards the picture of herself and her husband on the wall. "Robert's been gone for years, but I still miss him."

"How long were you married?" Penelope asked, walking over to look at the photograph with her.

"Unfortunately, only two years," Jeanne said. "He died in a boating accident not long after this picture was taken."

"Oh, I had no idea. I'm so sorry, Jeanne," Penelope said, placing her hand gently on the older woman's shoulder.

"Thank you, dear," Jeanne said, patting the top of Penelope's hand with her soft palm. She pulled in a sharp breath and blew it out quickly. "People say everything is meant to be, but I've never understood that sentiment. How is it meant to be that my husband dies in an accident? Maybe it's what I deserved, after all that time, loving him all of those years before we were finally able to be together, to be married. And then he was gone, just like that. Maybe God took him from me to teach me a lesson, take me down a peg."

"I'm sure it wasn't some kind of punishment, Jeanne. No one can explain why tragedies happen, why some lives are cut short," Penelope said.

"You're very sweet, dear," Jeanne said.

"Excuse me, Jeanne?" The young server from the restaurant poked his head in the doorway. He was dressed in his bartending uniform, ready to serve at the Happiest Hour. "Sorry to interrupt, but they have a question for you in the kitchen."

"It's okay," Jeanne said, turning to Penelope. "Will you be joining us, dear?"

Penelope nodded and watched her go, then returned her gaze to the photograph of Jeanne and Robert on the boat. It looked like it'd been enhanced. The bright colors reminded Penelope of the Technicolor movies she came across on the classic movie channel. Jeanne wore bright red lipstick, oversized

Jackie O sunglasses, a blue and yellow striped shirt and white pants. Robert sported a sailing cap and a blue ascot around his neck that matched the blue of Jeanne's shirt. They looked happy. Penelope couldn't help but wonder about the accident.

"Hey, Penelope," a voice called from the doorway.

Penelope turned and saw Lizzanne, one of Shane's production assistants. Her skin was crisp with sunburn, heat radiating from her freckled cheeks.

"Hi," Penelope said. "You ready to get back to work tomorrow? It looks like you got some sun this weekend."

"A little," Lizzanne said, glancing at her forearms. "Shane asked me to come in here and take pictures of the bookshelves. We're filming in here this week and he wants to know what books he'll have to get rid of."

Penelope laughed. "He's going to have to remove all of them or CGI them out. There aren't any books in here that date back to 1890."

"I guess," Lizzanne said, holding her iPhone sideways and snapping a series of pictures of the shelves. "Who knows, maybe he can just shoot away from them, make it work somehow. If nothing is bright pink or whatever maybe he can just blur them."

Penelope thought that might be distracting to the movie viewers but kept quiet. "Jeanne's okay with us filming in the library?"

"I think so. It might be a little inconvenient, but production is paying her an additional per diem. We're all staying here, but she's also getting a location contract out of the deal since we're using that suite upstairs for principal filming." Lizzanne snapped a few more pictures. "He's definitely going to have to take out that one that clearly says '1968.' That would mess up continuity for sure, out us on one of those movie-fail websites."

Penelope glanced up at the top shelf and saw the book she was talking about. "That looks like a high school yearbook." Pulling it from the shelf she ran her finger down the imprinted blue leather cover, which was embossed with an abstract image of a panther baring its teeth, the year 1968 stamped in an arc above it.

"Whoa, that's an antique," Lizzanne said, looking over Penelope's shoulder.

"Not quite. Vintage maybe," Penelope said. "I'm afraid to ask, but what year did you graduate high school?"

"1995," Lizzanne responded cheerfully. "Let's look at the funky hairstyles. Wait, wasn't everyone a hippie back then?"

"I don't think everyone was," Penelope said, carefully opening the book to a random page in the middle. The distinctive smell of aging paper wafted from the book as she gingerly turned the pages.

"Not a lot of hippies in here," Lizzanne said, "but there are some beehives. That's awesome. Look at that one." She pointed to a photo of a nice-looking girl wearing thick-rimmed black glasses. Her hair had been teased and sprayed into a tall pile on her head, a small bow tucked in the front of it. "I wish that look would come back."

"That looks like a lot of work," Penelope said. She leafed past the class photos to the clubs and activities section, finally landing on the section entitled "Homecoming." There she found a full-page color picture of the king and queen and their court standing on a stage. A beautiful girl with long black hair stood in a full-length sparkly dress. A small tiara perched on top of her head and a sash was draped over her shoulder declaring her Homecoming Queen. She wore long silk gloves that reached her elbows and one hand rested in the crooked elbow of the Homecoming King, who beamed proudly as he gazed at her.

Penelope imagined everyone at the dance being mesmerized by her beauty. She was simply stunning. Penelope thought she looked familiar and tried to place where she might have seen her, attempting to imagine this teenage girl's features on an older face of someone in town. She glanced down at the caption under the photo and realized why she looked familiar. She read out loud, "'Josephine Michaels and Robert Daniels lead the Homecoming Court for the Class of 1968.' This must be Josie Daniels. Her picture is up over the bar at the Shrimp Shack."

Lizzanne looked closer. "Yeah, I've seen it."

Penelope held the yearbook closer, looking at Josie's date. Then her eyes flicked to the oversized picture of Jeanne and her husband on the back of the boat on the wall. "Jeanne said her husband's name was Robert." Penelope studied the man's hairline and chin in both photos. "Does that look like the same guy to you?"

"Maybe," Lizzanne said tentatively. "It's hard to tell from black and white. Also, Jeanne's last name is Haverford. I deliver the daily paperwork and I've seen it a bunch of times."

Penelope shrugged. "Maybe Jeanne never changed her name. She said it was a short marriage. If this is the same Robert, Jeanne and Josie were both married to him."

Lizzanne took a closer look at Josie's picture in the yearbook. "She's beautiful."

"Was beautiful," Penelope said. "She died young, a long time ago." She glanced once again at the photo on the wall. "That seems to happen a lot around here."

Penelope turned a few more pages and found several featuring candid shots of students and teachers around the school, in classrooms and participating in extracurricular activities.

"Check out the bellbottoms," Lizzanne said with a laugh. "Those have made a comeback, but not as wide-legged as these. Look at them." She pointed to a picture of four girls sitting on top of a picnic table at the beach. They were dressed alike in wide-legged bellbottom jeans and matching tank tops with the panther logo from the yearbook on them, their arms linked together at the elbows as they smiled for the camera. Penelope recognized Josie second from the left next to a pretty girl with straight blonde hair, a wide middle part and thick round glasses, like the ones John Lennon wore. The two other girls had similar hairstyles with thick long tresses in varying colors, brushed out and frizzed up in the humid Florida air.

Penelope read the caption. "'Henrietta Miller, Josephine Michaels, Elizabeth Haverford and Rose Marie Jones head up the Blue and White Society.' Maybe Elizabeth is Jeanne's sister. It's hard to tell," Penelope said, glancing up at the photo of Jeanne on the wall and back to the smaller black and white one in the book. "I do see a resemblance, but this picture isn't the best quality. I'm pretty sure that's Rose though. The lady who runs the beach shop on the avenue."

Lizzanne nodded and asked, "What's a Blue and White Society?"

Penelope shrugged.

"I think blue and white are the school's colors. They're on the sign in front of the school complex, the one with the panther on it. Maybe they were in some kind of spirit club or something." Glancing at the picture on the opposite page she saw a male teacher standing in front of a classroom smiling at his students, appearing to be mid-lecture with his hands raised in a questioning shrug. He wore a wide tie and a short-sleeved dress shirt, his long bangs brushed across his forehead. The caption under the picture read, "Mr. Wainwright, Winner of

Favorite Teacher Award and School Club Advisor, Class of 1968."

"He looks like a hip dude. Cute, in a retro Ryan Reynolds kind of way. I'm sure the girls liked him," Lizzanne said. She stepped away and started scrolling through the pictures she'd taken on her phone. "I better get these off to Shane. See you later."

Penelope said goodbye distractedly as she turned a few more pages in the yearbook.

"Penny," Joey said from the doorway, startling her back to the present. He entered the library and kissed her on the cheek. "You ready?"

Penelope closed the yearbook and slid it back in its place on the top shelf. "Yes, let's go."

CHAPTER 17

Jeanne's cocktail party was well attended. Faint music played from behind the small bar while her guests milled about, drinking and snacking on hors d'oeuvres. Penelope saw about half of the attendees were Jeanne's friends and the other half were from the movie crew. The views from the roof of the Inn were magnificent, displaying the ocean for what seemed like hundreds of miles on end. A few people lounged underneath the canopy Jeanne kept on the patio for those who wanted to escape the direct sunlight.

Joey handed her a glass of chilled Sauvignon Blanc, a thin sheen of condensation already clinging to it. He held a beer in one hand and rested the other lightly on the railing, gazing out at the ocean.

"I had an interesting conversation with an old classmate," Penelope said, pulling him over to the patio railing.

"Really? You got in touch with one of your friends from school?" Joey asked, his interest piqued.

"Summer Farrington, power chef de cuisine in Manhattan," Penelope said, nodding and taking a sip of wine.

"Was she able to make you feel better about things?" Joey asked.

"No, just the opposite. She says she and Emilio were

involved back in school. Sexually involved," Penelope said, lowering her voice.

Joey put his hand on her shoulder and squeezed. "Sorry, Penny."

"It's funny, because that was always the rumor, so I shouldn't be shocked by what she said. But it's somehow more real to me now that I've heard it directly from her. It's not just whispers between classes now."

"You never talked to her about it back at school? After Emilio left?" Joey asked, looking out over the ocean.

Penelope shook her head. "She never said a word to me, or anyone, I don't think. That was part of the deal. She told me now because I let her believe he'd done something with me too...I didn't come out and lie, just implied something had happened."

"I know you've got to be disappointed in him," Joey said. "But also keep in mind, in those kinds of situations, it's he said, she said. She's not claiming rape or anything like that, right?"

Penelope choked a little on her wine and shook her head again. "No, and she was over the legal age of consent. His actions were improper, not criminal. But he should have known teachers aren't supposed to get involved with their students. Especially in a place like that, where they hold so much power over how well you do and where you end up after you graduate, career-wise."

"So taking into account what Summer says happened, we now have even more evidence of Emilio's lack of good judgment."

"Summer also said Christine Sullivan might have moved to Vermont. Did you have any luck tracking her down?"

"I haven't heard back from my partner back home yet, but I'll text him. The Vermont lead might help." Joey pulled his phone from his jacket and typed on the screen.

Penelope sighed and glanced at the doorway, waving over Max and Arlena who had just stepped onto the upper deck. Arlena conferred with Max for a second, then weaved her way through the crowd, joining them while Max headed to the bar. She wore a simple black jumpsuit with flared pants and silver high-heeled sandals.

"Hello, Pen, Joey," Arlena said, hugging Penelope around her shoulders. Joey slipped his phone back in his pocket.

"How did everything go today with Sienna?" Penelope asked, grateful for a change of topic.

"Perfectly. She's very innovative, and she's not afraid to tell me when my ideas aren't working."

Max sidled up, handing Arlena a glass of white wine. Dressed casually in dark slacks and a pale grey dress shirt opened at the collar, he took a sip from his beer bottle, scanning the crowd. "This sure is a sharp-looking group."

"Jeanne doesn't enforce a dress code, but it's sort of an unwritten rule. She says she likes to bring a little elegance to the beach," Penelope said.

"I can get behind that vibe," Max said. He spotted Shane leaning against the other end of the railing and went to introduce himself.

"You guys are working inside all day tomorrow?" Penelope asked Arlena. "They want us to set up in the Inn's parking lot for service."

"Yes, we're shooting a scene in the library. Max will be in the background," Arlena said, looking down the railing at Max. He was leaning against the railing and talking with Shane, who gestured excitedly with his hands as he spoke.

"Look who decided to join the party," Joey said, an edge coming into his voice.

Penelope turned and saw Emilio coming through the

doorway, leading Dominique by the hand. He paused to scan the deck, and then strode directly over to Shane and Max. The noise level of the crowd died down as people turned to watch them pass.

Gavin and Sienna entered next, squinting into the setting sun and then joining Arlena at the railing. The noise level of the party was increasing with more people arriving every minute. Penelope looked around for Jeanne and saw her talking with an older couple next to the bar, smiling and laughing. But Penelope could sense a nervous tension in her gestures. Penelope excused herself and walked over to the bar.

"Hi, Jeanne, great party," Penelope said.

"Oh, thank you, dear," Jeanne said anxiously. "I hope we don't run out of food."

Penelope glanced at the table. The platters were still about half full, the pigs in a blanket the most popular item. "I think you'll be fine. I can always call my guys and have them open up the kitchen truck downstairs. We can serve everyone tacos in a pinch."

Joey came up from behind and handed Penelope a fresh glass of wine.

"That would be something else, wouldn't it?" Jeanne said gratefully. "We may have to try that one time and see how it goes."

"Maybe for the wrap party after filming. I can talk to Shane. We can even invite people from the island to thank them for their hospitality—"

Penelope's planning was interrupted by a loud shout and the sound of shattering glass. Emilio was standing close to Shane, his cheeks bright red with anger and his finger pointing against Shane's chest. Max stood near them, a stunned look on his face. Dominique attempted to step between the two men, but was ignored by both of them as they stared each other down.

Suddenly Emilio grabbed Shane by the shirt and hoisted him onto the railing, teetering on the small of his back, his head dangling over the edge.

"Don't!" Shane cried. Dominique grabbed one of Emilio's arms while Max grabbed the other in an attempt to pull Shane back from the edge.

The crowd began to panic. Penelope felt Joey's body go rigid next to her. He set down his drink and walked quickly to the railing, pushing his way through the terrified onlookers.

"I told you I'd kill you," Emilio said. "I told you I would."

Joey yelled to him, "Let him go, Emilio. Bring him back down."

Shane howled, "Somebody help me! He's crazy! Help!"

Joey eased Dominique's hands from Emilio's arm and took her place, working with Max on the other side to pull him and Shane back over the railing. Shane kicked his legs in panic, landing blows on Emilio's lower limbs.

"Stop kicking," Joey said to him as he struggled with Emilio. He made eye contact with Max and started counting. On three, they pulled Emilio as hard as they could, dragging him backwards. Shane's head bounced against the railing before he fell in a heap onto the deck.

Emilio shook Max and Joey off and spun around, storming towards the door, awestruck onlookers parting to let him pass. Penelope noticed most of the crowd averted their eyes as he passed but she glared directly at him. He glanced briefly in her direction and Penelope saw that he was still enraged, but was surprised to see he looked hopelessly sad also. Dominique rushed after him, calling his name.

Joey and Max helped Shane into a deck chair and the crowd began to settle down. The bartender wrapped some ice in a towel and handed it to Shane, who held it gingerly to the back of his head. Max went to check on Arlena and Joey soothed a visibly distraught Jeanne. Only a few guests remained, staring at Shane as they finished their drinks and scarfed up the remaining appetizers. Penelope sat down in the chair next to Shane and asked him what had started the fight.

Shane looked at Penelope in disbelief. "He's crazy, that's what happened."

"Why did he attack you? Did something go wrong at the restaurant meeting today?" Penelope asked.

"It's a misunderstanding. He'll cool off and everything will be fine." Shane stood up unsteadily and made his way to the door. He turned back to her, frustration pinching his features. "Get down there early tomorrow. No one is allowed to be late. We've still got a movie to make."

Penelope watched Joey sit Jeanne down, holding her hand in his and speaking quietly to her. She looked over at Max and Arlena, who stood with Gavin and Sienna. They were all taking in the aftermath of the party with vague interest.

"Max, what happened over there?" Penelope asked after she rejoined them.

Max shook his head, "I don't know, one minute they're talking about the color of the booth benches at their new place and the next minute that Emilio guy is going *Full Metal Jacket* on Shane, trying to lob him off the side of the building. That dude's got a short fuse."

"What did Shane say to set him off?" Penelope asked.

"I don't know. Something about the house he's rebuilding. Shane said he stayed there and there was a leak in the upstairs bathroom, and that he should use the same plumber they're using for the restaurant. The next minute Emilio yanks the beer from Shane's hand, smashes it on the floor and grabs him by the shirt," Max said. "I was actually getting bored with their conversation until, well, *that* happened."

Joey rejoined the conversation and thanked Max for his help.

"How is Jeanne doing?" Penelope asked.

"She's pretty upset," Joey said. "Emilio should watch himself. He's out on bail, but an assault charge will get him locked up again."

"Do you think Shane is going to press charges?" Penelope asked. "He didn't seem like he wanted to. They're business partners in the middle of closing a big deal."

"I have no idea," Joey said. "If he doesn't want to there's not much the police can do."

Penelope noticed Jeanne had left. The server was on bended knee, sweeping up the shattered glass.

Arlena decided to head back to the boat, saying she'd had enough excitement for one evening. Gavin suggested the rest of them grab something for dinner.

"I'm up for that," Sienna said. "Cocktail hour was exciting. I can't wait to see what's in store for supper."

CHAPTER 18

Joey and Penelope declined the dinner invitation, deciding instead to keep their original plans. Penelope stopped in her room before they left for Joey's cabin to grab her backpack, tossing in a toothbrush and a change of clothes.

Back downstairs, she poked her head into the library on her way to the lobby. Jeanne was in there alone, the lights dimmed and a glass of amber liquor in a tumbler on the table next to her chair. She faced out towards the windows, drinking quietly.

Penelope knocked lightly on the door before entering, so as not to startle her. "Jeanne, are you okay?" Even in the darkness, Penelope could see her cheeks were wet with tears.

Penelope walked over and eased herself down gently in the adjoining chair. "This is the second time today I've found you in here crying by yourself," Penelope said. "Are you upset about us being here? Are we disrupting your life too much?"

Jeanne laughed and shook her head. "Well, that was quite a commotion up there this evening, wasn't it? But for the most part, no. I've loved having you all here, bringing new life and excitement to this old place."

"We've enjoyed it too. Thanks for opening up your home."

Jeanne swirled her glass. "I grew up here, watching visitors and tourists come and go my whole life. It goes by so quickly.

But I must say, having a movie filmed here...well, that's the most exciting thing that's happened in a long time."

"Why are you upset then?" Penelope asked.

"It's nothing, dear. Sometimes I get overwhelmed by everything that's happened in my life, like all of the bad things are my doing. And when those girls went missing...I fear it's my fault, that I've invited something unsettling onto the island," she said, her voice falling to a whisper. "When Shane contacted me about coming here and using the Inn, I jumped at the chance. I've never been one to think change is bad. How could filming an elegant historical movie be an evil thing?"

Penelope tried to follow Jeanne's line of reasoning.

"How could what happened to Rebekkah and Sabena be your fault?"

Jeanne sighed. "None of you would be here if it weren't for me agreeing to the movie. I fought against some members of the city council to help get the permits, argued with the residents who said you'd be a burden on our resources, would disrupt the tourist season." She snorted harshly. "I own the only hotel on the island and people were worried about losing money on the tourists."

Penelope thought for a minute. "Who was against us coming, specifically?"

"You missed a lot of it in the beginning, before you got here," Jeanne said. "When the production company sent out the location scouts, and we really started sitting down to discuss how we could make this work, we got a lot of opposition from the community."

"Really? What happened?" Penelope asked.

"Everyone from the principal of the school to the marina owner to the town manager showed up for the city council meeting and had a say. They were mostly concerned about the disruption to the island, overcrowding the beach, loss of revenue and tourism."

"I haven't run into anyone who made me feel unwelcome," Penelope said. "I've heard rumblings from a few of the crew about some less-than-pleasant residents, but you get that wherever you go. A film crew takes up a lot of space, that's just the nature of what we do."

"Well, it's not everyone on the island, of course, but enough. Rose was one of the first people to throw up a fuss about you all," Jeanne sniffed. "She hated the idea of a movie crew coming here. Too many strangers, she said. But she changed her tune when you booked up most of her cabins for the summer. I shouldn't say, it's none of my business, but I know she upped her rates when the production company contacted her. I guess she figured she'd at least make a nice profit once you got here."

"I guess that's fair," Penelope said. "She probably had to turn away some regular summer rentals because of us."

"True. I had to also. Rose has always had a good mind for business," Jeanne said with a little laugh. "Do you know she charges her renters fifty dollars if they lose their cabin keys? You know it costs less than five dollars to get a key made over on the mainland." Jeanne took another sip of her drink and stood up from her chair. "I'm going to head up to my apartment and go to bed. I'll be more cheerful in the morning."

"Okay," Penelope said. "My crew is getting started in the parking lot pretty early. I hope we don't disturb you too much."

"It's fine, dear. I'll be getting up anyway." Jeanne gave her a little wave and left the library, a little wobbly on her feet. Penelope waited a moment and then followed her out.

CHAPTER 19

Penelope was the first one on set the next morning. Waking up before sunrise was difficult, especially the first day after a long break. She had slept over at Joey's cabin, murmuring a sleepy goodbye to him and kissing his ear before slipping out around four thirty in the morning. Waves crashed next to her, her feet sinking soothingly into the sand with each step she made toward the Inn. For just a moment, Penelope felt like she was all alone in the world, that she was the only person awake on the entire island. She'd treasured the silence, knowing the day ahead would be full of noise and chaos on set.

The Inn's parking lot, now canopied with tents, would double as her kitchen and dining room for most of the coming week. A pile of long collapsible tables was stacked high in one corner. She pulled the top one down, straightening the legs and setting it up in the front of the tent. She arranged a few more into a large square, setting up the prep area for her chefs.

A few minutes later Penelope heard the backup warning signal and saw the glowing red taillights of her kitchen truck easing into the far corner of the parking lot. She stepped out of the tent and watched Francis and Quentin step down from the cab. They exchanged greetings.

"Where are the others?" Penelope said.

"They're right behind us in the pantry truck," Francis said. They both looked rested and energetic, ready to jump on the prep work for the day.

Penelope walked around the truck, performing a quick inspection, checking the gas and water lines. The trucks had been parked in the high school lot during the long weekend and she wanted to be sure nothing had come loose during transit. Or that they hadn't been tampered with by any curious visitors.

Her crew set in motion, Penelope climbed into the cab of the kitchen truck, which doubled as her office, and began finalizing the menus for the week.

Breakfast came and went in a flash and one hundred and seventy-two people were fed. Afterwards they all dispersed, some of them heading to the makeup and wardrobe tent on the beach or back inside the Inn to get the first shot set up. Penelope stood in the middle of the tent after they'd all gone and surveyed the damage. "Not too bad," she said to herself. It would take them an hour or so to break down the breakfast stations, store the leftovers, wipe down the tables and wash the dishes before they could start getting lunch ready. Luckily Jeanne had a pretty nice industrial dishwasher inside that they were paying her to be able to use.

"Hi, Miss Sutherland," Regan said, entering the tent.

"Regan," Penelope said. "Good to see you. Ready to help us prep lunch?"

"Sure," Regan said. He walked over to a nearby table and gathered up a few stray cups and napkins.

"After you get the dishes done and restacked, why don't you work in the kitchen today? I'll tell Francis that you'll be shadowing him."

Regan paused and smiled widely. "Yeah, that will be great. Thanks." A spring came into his step as he quickly cleared the tables.

For lunch, Penelope and her team prepared grilled Chilean sea bass with mango salsa, roasted cilantro lime chicken breasts over saffron-infused rice and grilled flank steak, sliced thin and served with roasted new potatoes rubbed with olive oil and seasoned with fresh rosemary. Penelope looked in on Regan a few times as they worked. She noticed he listened intently to the other chefs and seemed eager to follow their directions.

Quentin and Penelope got the ice bins in position and worked on filling up the frosted bowls with various salad toppings, greens and sides, working side by side at one of the long prep tables. "Let's wait on bringing the ice out until they're actually breaking," Penelope said to him quietly. "You know how they are. I told them the same thing on the truck. I don't want them firing anything until the last minute."

Shane broke for lunch twenty minutes after the scheduled time, which wasn't too bad considering his usual delays. The first diners began trickling into the tent, expectant looks on their faces as they ogled the steam tables and salad bar. If by some chance Shane had called the break on time, she would've had a line of people waiting and a row of empty steam trays for them to admire. But her gamble had paid off, and she felt like for the first time they had appetizing food that hadn't been sitting for the better part of an hour while they waited. Arlena had wanted to read through her scenes for the rest of the day in private, so Penelope offered her the room upstairs, and had Arlena's lunch delivered there.

The actors started filing into the tent behind the first group of crew members. They were easy to pick out in their period costumes. The women wore dresses draped with beads and the men wool suits with matching fedoras. Penelope circled the room a few times, watching the actors tapping the glass screens of their phones, a jarring contrast to their clothes. Their heavy makeup gave them a sallow appearance, which made them look otherworldly.

Penelope heard yelling outside the tent and hurried over to see what the commotion was. Several curious diners had paused and were gazing out towards the parking lot.

"This is all your fault!" a woman shouted at Francis.

"Why don't you tell me what you're talking about," Francis said in a soothing tone.

"What's going on?" Penelope asked, stepping outside and recognizing Roni Lambert, Sabena's mother. Her face was bright red below her blonde bangs and she looked like she hadn't slept in days.

"I don't know, Boss. She just came up here and started yelling," Francis said, lifting his shoulders under his chef coat.

"It's you! You're the one," Mrs. Lambert spat in Penelope's direction. "You did this to her."

Penelope's heart started beating rapidly. "Mrs. Lambert, what do you mean?"

Mrs. Lambert lunged at Penelope but Francis grabbed her, holding her back gently by the shoulders. Mrs. Lambert gave up immediately and crumpled to the asphalt, sobbing into her hands.

"What the hell is going on down here?" Shane yelled, his already high-pitched voice going up an octave. He stormed out of the back door of the Inn towards them. "Penelope, what are you doing? I'm trying to review our scenes from this morning and—who is this?" he demanded, pointing at Mrs. Lambert, who sat rocking back and forth on the ground at their feet.

"This is Sabena's mother," Penelope said. She glanced

behind her and saw that most of the people in the tent had gotten up from their chairs and stood silently behind her, watching what was happening.

Shane raised his hands in a questioning gesture. "Who?"

Penelope looked at him sharply. "Sabena Lambert. My server. This is her mother." She willed him to make the connection.

A look of recognition finally came to his face.

Mrs. Lambert stopped sobbing abruptly and looked up, noticing the crowd of people watching her from the tent. She pulled herself back onto her feet, Francis officering her a hand. She slapped it away and rocked on her heels. The warm asphalt left an imprint on her thigh and she brushed sand from her leg. "You all come in here and take over, with your promises of fame, money, trying to make something different out of our kids. And now she's dead because of you."

Penelope's knees wobbled beneath her. "Sabena is dead?" she whispered harshly.

Mrs. Lambert glared at Penelope, squaring her shoulders. "Bean is dead. There was nothing the doctors could do. My baby never woke up." Her face crumpled into a sob, and she held her face in her hands.

No one said anything as they watched. Penelope looked at Shane with a questioning glance, which he returned with a shrug.

"Mrs. Lambert," Penelope said, taking a step towards her. "We are all so sorry to hear about Sabena."

Mrs. Lambert did not look up and continued whimpering, her shoulders shuddering under her faded t-shirt. Penelope took another step and reached out, placing a hand gingerly on the woman's shoulder. Mrs. Lambert's head jerked up and she shrugged Penelope's hand away. Before Penelope could react,

Mrs. Lambert shoved her hard in the chest, pushing her back into the crowd of onlookers, who thankfully caught her before she fell to the asphalt.

"You keep your hands off me, bitch," Mrs. Lambert spat at her. "You're all going to pay for this. I promise you that. You," she pointed at Penelope, "and you," she said, pointing at Shane. "You both think you're better than everybody, but you're not. Corrupting our kids with your drugs and your booze and your Hollywood nonsense, filling their heads with crazy ideas."

Francis moved closer to her, ready to grab her if she made another move towards Penelope.

"I'll see you both in court. I'll ruin you. Who do you think is going to go see a movie made by a bunch of murderers? I'll make sure everyone knows what you've done," Mrs. Lambert said, wiping tears angrily from her face. And with that she turned to go, her flip flops slapping loudly against her heels as she walked back down to the avenue.

"Should I go after her?" Francis asked.

"For what? Just let her go," Shane said. He stood with his hands on his hips.

Francis shrugged. "She assaulted one of our crew. You okay?" he asked, glancing at Penelope.

Penelope nodded. "I'm okay." Her hands were shaking and her heart hadn't slowed to its normal pace, but she wasn't injured. She turned and thanked the people who had caught her and walked unsteadily over to Shane. The crowd began to break up, mumbling about the scene they'd just witnessed.

"Shane," Penelope said. "Maybe we should take a break or call it a day. A crew member has died."

"What?" Shane laughed, genuinely amused. "Are you crazy? Look at all of those people in there," he said, pointing to the tent. "They're dressed, made up and ready to go. We've got five more hours of work today at least. You want me to call it a day because a part-time waitress decided to party too hard and couldn't handle it? No way."

"But—" Penelope began.

"But what? And where do you get off advising me on anything? You're the caterer. I could replace you tomorrow and no one would notice. Don't get in my face about anything ever again or you're off the movie." Shane stormed back inside the Inn, slamming the door behind him.

Penelope stood stunned, going over Shane's words in her mind.

"He's outta line, Boss," Francis said. "It's his show, but he shouldn't talk to you like that."

Penelope nodded but didn't look at him, her cheeks burning red. She walked over to the truck and took off her chef jacket, placed it on the seat of the cab and closed the door before heading towards Ocean Avenue.

"Boss, where are you going?" Francis said, jogging after her, a look of concern on his face.

Penelope shook her head and put her hands on her hips, feeling tension all the way down her back. "I'm taking a walk," she said, pulling her sunglasses from the pocket of her baggy chef pants and putting them on. "You're in charge. Do me a favor and finish service, get everything cleaned up."

"Okay, Boss, no problem," Francis said. "Anything you need, call me."

Penelope thanked him quickly and walked off, heading south down Ocean Avenue.

CHAPTER 20

Penelope seethed as she walked, furious at Shane for speaking to her the way he did. When the anger began to wear off, it was replaced by a feeling she couldn't quite describe. It was something like sadness, mixed with anxiety and fear. Glancing out at the perfect blue ocean, the gold sunlight dancing on the waves, she wondered how she could be feeling such a toxic cocktail of emotions in such a beautiful place. Penelope had never walked off of a set during filming. She'd never called in sick and she was rarely ever late. Priding herself on her strong work ethic, she was usually the first one on and the last one off a set during filming. She had a strange floating feeling, like she was skipping school or had run away from home.

She walked past Rose's place without even looking inside. Penelope always stopped to at least wave hello to Rose, but she wasn't in the mood to be social. When she came to the empty building that was supposed to one day be Craw Daddy's she saw that the door was padlocked and the police tape across the doors fluttered in the warm breeze. Seeing the building brought on another wave of sadness and Penelope quickly looked away.

She walked into Josie's Shrimp Shack and took a seat at the empty bar, propping her forearms on the cool wood.

"What can I get for you?" Jonny Daniels emerged from the kitchen and stepped behind the bar.

Penelope said, "A beer."

Jonny laughed and looked at the long row of beer taps. "Anything specific?" He hooked a long strand of black hair behind his ear and smiled at her.

"Surprise me," Penelope sighed. The adrenaline had worn off after the incident with Mrs. Lambert and now she was feeling uncharacteristically tired.

Jonny drummed his fingers on the bar for a second then poured her a lager in a frosted pint glass.

Penelope thanked him and drank her beer in silence.

"You're Miss Sutherland, from the movie, right? Regan's boss?"

Penelope nodded tightly and drank another gulp, wiping foam from her lip. "That's me," she said sulkily.

"I saw you the other night talking to Regan and he told me later who you were. You guys finished early today, huh? Regan was saying he probably wouldn't be back until dinner."

"They're still working. I'm on break," Penelope said.

"Oh, okay. You want something to eat?" Jonny asked, looking around for a menu.

"No, thanks," Penelope said.

"Regan really loves working on a real movie set," Jonny said. He pulled a wet pint glass from a dish rack and began wiping it off with a bar towel, setting it next to some matching ones on a narrow shelf right behind the bar.

"He's a great cook," Penelope said. "He was up on the truck today, preparing the main courses."

"Cool. I know he wants to take on more responsibility," Jonny said, genuinely pleased.

Penelope thought for a minute and asked, "If Regan

decided he wanted to go into cooking full-time somewhere besides here, how would you feel about that?"

Jonny picked up another pint glass from the rack to dry. "If that's what he really wants to do, it's fine by me. But this place is pretty much the only kitchen on the island to work in, except for the Inn."

"How would you feel if he wanted to leave with us, come on the road with a theatrical catering crew, see more of the world?" Penelope asked.

Jonny paused a moment, thinking. "I'd be all for it, to tell you the truth. His mom would miss him, I'm sure. But if it made him happy, and he remembered to come home and visit once in a while...then I think we'd be okay with it."

"It's different here than anyplace I've been," Penelope said. "I was talking to Bradley about going off to college recently."

Jonny nodded. "Yeah, you'd like for your kids to stay, make a life close to you, but the options are limited. Which is part of the charm of the island, I guess."

Penelope drank her beer and fell silent.

"I'll be right back," Jonny said, eyeing her pint glass and heading out to help his customers seated outside.

Penelope slid off her stool and went to the ladies room while he was gone. When she returned to the main room, she stopped to look at the picture of Josie up over the bar.

Jonny walked back in, his arm loaded down with dirty plates. "That's my mom and me," he said, nodding up at the picture.

Penelope smiled. "You were a cute baby."

"Another?" he asked, eyeing her glass.

"Yes, please," Penelope said.

He returned to the bar and set a new frosted glass down in front of her.

"I saw a picture of your mom in a yearbook over at the Inn. She was Homecoming Queen?"

Jonny laughed. "Yeah, I've seen that picture. She and Dad were pretty decked out."

"So your parents met in high school?" Penelope asked, relaxing slightly.

Jonny nodded. "I think they knew each other growing up on the island, but I heard that Dad didn't really notice Mom until high school. Then he pulled all these crazy romantic stunts to get her attention, leaving flowers at her house, stuff like that."

"So they started this place together?" Penelope asked, looking around the Shrimp Shack at all of the old black and white photos.

"After high school they got married, had me and opened this place. It used to literally be just a shack on the beach when they started. We added on the deck and made other improvements over the years."

"It's a unique spot, that's for sure," Penelope said. "Jonny, if you don't mind me asking, what happened to your mom? I heard she passed away."

Jonny paused for a moment, his mood dipping a bit. "Unfortunately, she died in an accident. She didn't suffer, which is good."

Penelope thought Jonny's words sounded rehearsed, like he'd spoken them many times before. "I'm so sorry to hear that."

Jonny smiled wistfully. "Thanks. I was just a baby so I don't remember her. But that's what happened. And then my dad died a few years later. Also in an accident, on a boat out in the ocean. My family is very accident prone."

Penelope wasn't sure how to respond to his attempt at levity while discussing the deaths of his parents, so she just took another sip of beer.

"That one's going down quicker than the first one," Jonny said.

Penelope smiled and polished it off, setting her glass back on the coaster and shaking her head when he asked her if she wanted another.

"Was your dad by himself out on the boat when he..." Penelope trailed off.

"Died? Yes, he was out fishing, alone, and then he was gone. Fell overboard, is what I was told. Never found his body either. That can happen too, depending on the currents and how far out he was. Bad luck, really."

"That's so sad, Jonny, I'm sorry," Penelope said.

"It was a long time ago," Jonny said. "I've made my peace with it, and I've had a good life regardless."

"So your father remarried after your mom passed away?"

Jonny leaned on his fists on the shiny wood bar. "Yep. Got married to Jeanne from the Inn. That's how it went. They were all friends, back in school, a pretty tight-knit group."

"Are you and Jeanne close? She was your step-mom for a little while."

Jonny shrugged and smiled. "Sure, she's a sweet old lady. Honestly, all of that happened when I was really little. By the time I got to school, everything had settled down. All the tragedy was behind me."

Penelope nodded and took another sip of her beer.

"You guys can sit anywhere," Jonny said to a group of four that came through the front door. They opted for a patio seat and he went out to get them settled.

Penelope's phone pinged in her back pocket and she reluctantly pulled it out to look at the screen. There was a text from Francis that read, "All good here. Lunch is cleared. Restocking the trucks now." Penelope sighed and put the phone facedown on the bar without responding and stared at the small puddle of froth resting in the bottom of her glass. After a few minutes Penelope groaned inwardly and turned her phone back over, swiping it to life. She responded, "Thanks, Francis. Heading back in a few to help close up."

CHAPTER 21

Penelope walked back down Ocean Avenue to the Inn, feeling much more relaxed than when she headed to Josie's. She still felt a feeling of dread somewhere deep down, something tugging at the back of her mind, in her gut. She thought about Jonny's parents both dying so young and shivered, folding her arms loosely over her chest. As she passed by Emilio's empty building she saw him standing outside on the sidewalk, staring up at the roof. When he saw her approaching, his shoulders dipped and he put his hands on his hips.

"Chef," Penelope said tightly. He looked exhausted, like he'd been up all night.

Emilio shook his head and studied his shoes. "Here we go again. You know, I think the biggest mistake I made was stepping foot on this little strip of sand. This island is beautiful when you look at it from the outside, but I think once you're inside it might actually be Hell on earth."

"Are you sure that's the biggest mistake you've ever made?" Penelope asked sarcastically. "I can think of a couple more."

"What are you talking about?" Emilio snapped at her.

"I think you know. I talked to Summer. I know what you two did back in school, you can stop lying about it now," Penelope said, letting the disgust she felt slip into her voice.

"I've already told you a million times, nothing happened between me and that little liar, or anyone else," Emilio said.

Penelope took a step closer to him and glared. "Watch your mouth. You can't talk about her that way."

"I can if she's going to keep lying about me," Emilio countered. "She's not supposed to be saying anything anyway. If she keeps it up, I can get my money back."

"What money?" Penelope asked.

"The settlement she got from me and the school. I had to pay out part of my severance to her. You'd think that would be enough...got her set up in a nice apartment in the city; heard she has a great job too."

"Chef, tell me to my face, and don't lie, or leave anything out. Did you sleep with Summer Farrington back at school?"

Emilio pulled his sunglasses from his face and closed the gap between them. "No, I never touched her. Or the other girl."

"Christine," Penelope said, not breaking the stare. "Her name is Christine."

"Yeah, Christine," Emilio said, looking away first. He sighed and stepped away from her, leaning against his empty restaurant space.

After a few minutes of silence Emilio said, "Let's see," he started ticking items off on his thick fingers. "My favorite former student thinks I'm a perv, the future of my restaurant is up in the air because dealing with these island locals is a nightmare, my business partner has been taking showers in my bathroom and don't forget the little detail about me being accused of kidnapping two teenage girls. I've gone from the top of the world to rock bottom in the space of a few days."

Penelope shifted her weight and looked down at her feet. "Shane has been taking showers in your bathroom?"

"Yeah, he let it slip at that party yesterday that there was a leak in the bathroom upstairs. Yeah, there's a leak in the bathroom, in the master suite shower that he has no business being in."

"So that's why you attacked him?" Penelope asked.

"Skinny little bastard, trying to step in my shoes, while I'm in jail, no less. In jail for something I didn't do, by the way," Emilio reminded her. He was overheated and angry, and Penelope kept her distance.

"So, besides the leak in the shower, do you have any proof Shane and Dominique are having an affair?" Penelope asked carefully.

"No," Emilio admitted. "She denies it, of course. Dominique says she asked him to stay over at the house because she's afraid to sleep out there by herself. But she said he slept downstairs on the couch. So how would he know about the leak?"

"She told me the same thing, that she didn't like being in the house alone at night," Penelope said. "Did she have an explanation for him knowing about the leak?"

"Yeah, she says she asked him to take a look at it the next morning, to see if it was okay for her to take a shower." A fresh wave of anger seemed to wash over him. "She never even told me she asked him to sleep over. Why would she keep that from me? They're obviously hiding something."

"Chef, maybe it's as simple as what she's saying. I saw your reaction at the party. Maybe she just didn't want to make you angry over something that has an innocent explanation. Don't you trust Dominique?"

"Of course I trust her. It's him I don't trust. I see the way he looks at her. At all women. He acts like such a tough guy, but I know how he really is. He's afraid of appearing weak and that makes him angry," Emilio said.

"Look," Penelope said, feeling a surprising wave of pity for her former teacher wash over her. "It's not my place to say, but if you believe your wife, you should trust her too. Can you let the thing with Shane go?"

"But how am I supposed to let it go? Shane is entwined in our lives now. We're married to him, with this restaurant and partnership, all the papers I've signed. If everything goes south, I'll never be able to pay back the money he's put up for this." He waved at the empty building.

"You have to trust you made the right move, Chef," Penelope said. "And if you haven't, you'll have to make another choice to make it right."

Emilio's phone rang in his back pocket and he pulled it out to look at the screen. "Hello," he said after glancing at the number. "Yes, I'm at the restaurant." He put the phone down and looked at her. "That was my attorney. Because Sabena Lambert died this morning and they're amending the charge to negligent homicide." He shook his head and sat down slowly on a nearby bench. After appearing to be lost in thought for a moment, he said, "I told you. We're in Hell, Penelope."

CHAPTER 22

When Penelope returned to the Inn, the first person she saw was Max. He was standing on the front porch smoking a cigarette. When he saw Penelope he smiled and snuffed it in the sand in the large cement urn next to the railing. He was still in costume, although he'd removed his jacket and tie, which were hung across the porch railing. He came down the steps. "There you are. We've been worried about you." He pulled her into a hug and she breathed in the smell of smoke mixed with jasmine.

"Thanks, I needed that. Where is Arlena?" Penelope asked, stepping away from him.

"She's upstairs in your room. She's furious with Shane for going off on you in front of everyone. The whole crew was bummed out, really. Finding out that girl died and then seeing Shane act like he couldn't care less and laying into you kind of put a damper on the rest of the day. He wrapped early and sent us on our way a little while ago. Here comes Joey," Max said, nodding towards the avenue.

Penelope spun around quickly, the sun catching her eyes at the wrong moment. She closed them and saw red slashes against her eyelids.

Joey smiled tightly at Max and Penelope. "You guys still

working?" He walked over and put an arm around Penelope's waist.

"We're done for the day," Penelope said. "Let's head upstairs."

When they got to Penelope's room they found Arlena, Gavin and Sienna sitting on the balcony, bottles of water sweating on the table in front of them, their turn-of-the-century costumes laid across Penelope's bed. Their faces hadn't been scrubbed of their heavy pancake makeup yet, which made them look pale and sickly in the natural light.

Arlena hugged Penelope tightly when she entered. "Shane is a bastard and I told him so. I demanded he apologize to you in front of the whole crew tomorrow or I'd walk. Gavin backed me up," she said, glancing back out through the glass doors.

"Thanks, Arlena," Penelope said. "That means a lot."

"What happened?" Joey asked, concern flooding his face.

Penelope filled him in on the scene downstairs, her voice hitching slightly when she got to the part about Mrs. Lambert blaming her for Sabena's death. When she finished Penelope sat down on the edge of the bed, careful to avoid the costumes.

A muscle worked in Joey's jaw, then his expression softened.

"I'm sorry you had to go through that."

Penelope fought down a lump of emotion, refusing to cry in front of her friends and coworkers. She stood up quickly from the bed and grabbed a bottle of water from the mini refrigerator.

Gavin and Sienna came in from the balcony and Gavin said, "There she is, the voice of reason on the set."

"Gav, let's go and leave Penelope alone. We're crowding her in her own room," Sienna said quietly, lacing her fingers in his.

"I appreciate your support, all of you," Penelope said. "That's why Shane has the reputation that he has. He's a difficult genius of a director. We'll all be over it and back to work by morning."

Penelope's phone pinged in her pocket and she pulled it out to read the new text message. It was from Quentin and it read, "911. Cops at the Inn. Want to talk to us again."

"This day isn't done with me yet," Penelope said. "I've got to head downstairs."

CHAPTER 23

They all descended the wide staircase together into the main hallway. Detective Williams had arrived and was questioning Regan while Francis stood nervously nearby.

"Where's Quentin?" Penelope asked. "He just texted me."

"The rest of the guys are in the lot locking up the trucks. He said he was going to slip outside and get a hold of you."

"I had nothing to do with those girls after I dropped them off," Regan repeated. "I told you, I left them alone with that Emilio guy, watched them walk into his house and then I left."

"Excuse me, Detective," Penelope said, "I thought you already had Emilio under arrest. Why are you asking Regan about Friday night again?"

"We still have some questions about the timeline of the night in question, ma'am," Detective Williams said, turning back to Regan. "You said you came back through town on Ocean Avenue and then went home." He consulted his notebook and glanced back up at Regan.

Regan looked at him, his face reddening. "Yes. That's right."

"Well, I just spoke to your father and he stated you didn't come home Friday night. He said your car wasn't in the driveway all night and he didn't see you until later Saturday morning." Detective Williams spoke softly, in a conversational tone. "Why would your father tell us that, Mr. Daniels?"

Regan looked like he was going to be sick. Francis stepped closer to him and put a hand on his shoulder from behind to steady him. He recovered slightly. "Okay, I didn't go home right after." He looked at Penelope at the bottom of the stairs and then at the faces of the others who stood right behind her.

Officer Williams' voice hardened slightly. "Why don't you tell me what really happened on Friday night? Did you end up partying with those girls? Maybe you all had a little too much to drink and things got out of hand?"

"No." Regan shook his head forcefully. "No, I left them there and then I...decided to have a few beers by myself on the beach and I fell asleep."

Penelope looked over at Joey. His jaw was firmly set and he squeezed her hand when she took a step forward and started to speak. "Detective, I did see Regan early Saturday morning, alone, asleep outside of Rose's beach store."

Detective Williams glanced at her. "Are you sure about that, Miss Sutherland?"

Penelope nodded. "Yes. I saw him around seven thirty."

Detective Williams turned back to Regan. "Where were you in between the time when you dropped Sabena Lambert and Rebekkah Flores at the suspect's house until the time Miss Sutherland found you?"

"I told you, I was drinking and sleeping on the beach," Regan said, looking at his shoes.

"Are you sure you weren't partying with two underage girls and then padlocking them into a construction site after they passed out?" Detective Williams grilled. He moved further into Regan's space, edging closer as he spoke.

"No!" Regan said. "I would never hurt them, I swear."

His eyes glassed over; he looked to be on the verge of tears.

"Detective," Gavin said from behind Penelope. "Hold on a moment."

Penelope and Joey turned to Gavin, who stood next to Sienna, Max and Arlena on his other side.

"Regan was with me on Friday night. I can testify to his whereabouts and whatever else you may need," Gavin said, walking towards them.

"Excuse me, who are you?" Detective Williams asked.

Gavin glanced back at the crowd and smiled. "I'm Gavin McKenna, the as-yet-unknown actor from England, here to film this illustrious period movie on this crazy beach with my very talented friends."

Detective Williams leveled his gaze at Gavin. "So, you're saying he was with you on Friday night. With you where?"

"In my room upstairs," Gavin said. "All night."

Penelope glanced at Sienna, expecting her to be shocked or angry, but she only stood with the others with her serene smile still in place.

"Gav," Sienna said, stepping forward. "Why didn't you speak up sooner and save this young man the trauma?"

Gavin shook his head and put his arm over Regan's shoulders. "I'm sorry, Regan. I should have come to your defense before now. Please forgive me. As for you all," Gavin said to the silent and shocked group, "I guess the charade is over. And maybe my leading man career as well."

Detective Williams sighed. "So you have an alibi witness. But how do I know he's not lying for you?"

"Detective," Gavin said, "I just admitted to being gay in front of my coworkers and my fiancée. Well, she already knew. But really, you don't think I would just do that for no reason, do you?"

"I saw Regan's car in the parking lot that night," Jeanne said, stepping forward. "I did wonder at the time why it would be here. He usually parks at Rose's. But then I forgot all about it."

"Okay," Detective Williams said, slipping his notebook back into his pocket. "And you didn't go out at all after you got back to the Inn? You didn't happen to see anything out of the ordinary on Ocean Avenue?"

"No," Regan said, his gaze still on the floor, his voice just above a whisper. "I didn't see anything."

"My room faces out onto the ocean, Detective," Gavin said. "Lovely views, but none of the street side of the building."

Detective Williams nodded and turned to go. Everyone relaxed and began talking to each other in murmured tones.

"Detective," Penelope said, catching him in the doorway. "Is there any update on Rebekkah? Do you know how she's doing?"

He looked down at her and said, "She hasn't woken up yet, but her vital signs are stable. Of the two, she was in better shape when they were first brought in. The doctors are cautiously optimistic, but there's no way to tell when she'll come out of the coma."

Penelope thanked him and turned back to group, heading right over to Regan, who had slumped against the wall of the hallway. "Hey, how are you doing?"

He shrugged and said, "Okay, I guess. Relieved I'm not getting arrested right now, but I wasn't expecting to be outed in front of everyone." He shrugged and studied his shoes.

"Regan," Penelope said. "I'm glad you're okay. And it makes no difference to us. We care about you."

Regan looked at her with an expression of mild surprise and gratitude.

"Well, my secret is out now. I've felt so isolated for so long.

I don't know anyone else on the island who is gay. And then Gavin came along."

They looked over at Gavin, who was holding hands with Sienna again and talking with Max and Arlena.

"Do your parents know?" Penelope asked.

"No. I guess I should head over and talk to them before they hear it from someone else. News travels fast around here."

"Okay, see you tomorrow?" Penelope said.

Regan untied his apron and pulled it from his waist, folding it into a square. "Yeah, I'll be here."

"Regan, wait a minute," Gavin said, noticing he was about to walk out the front door. The two of them stepped outside on the front porch. Gavin spoke to Regan in a hushed voice, his hand on his shoulder. After a few minutes they hugged and Regan walked down the front steps to the avenue. Gavin came back inside and rejoined the group.

"Gavin, why didn't you tell us before now?" Arlena asked. "You know it doesn't matter, right?"

Gavin smiled and said, "You're lovely, Arlena, and it's true that it shouldn't matter. I always wanted to be out, but my manager and agent told me I should keep my sexuality quiet if I wanted to be considered a leading man and get any role I wanted."

"I think that's all changing now, Gavin," Max said. "It's not like people have to be untrue to themselves like in the old days, right?"

Gavin shrugged. "I guess so. I hope so. Well, I'll be the example now, won't I? We'll see how my career goes after this all comes to light."

"So the wedding's off?" Sienna jokingly pouted.

Gavin laughed.

"I suppose it is. You're free to go."

"I'll never go too far from you," Sienna said, kissing his cheek.

"I need a drink," Gavin said. "I'm heading up to the roof. Care to join us?"

Arlena and Max agreed and they all headed upstairs.

"You coming, Pen?" Max asked, looking back over his shoulder.

Penelope glanced at Joey and said, "I don't think so. Not tonight."

"Okay, see you tomorrow," Max said and caught up with the others.

Penelope looked at Joey and said, "What do you want to do tonight?"

Joey shook his head and said, "I have no plans, Penny Blue. What would you like to do?"

"Come up to my room while I change and we'll think about it," she said, turning to go up the stairs.

CHAPTER 24

When they got to Penelope's room, Joey stepped out onto the balcony while Penelope took a quick shower and changed into a dark blue sundress. She opened her mini fridge and pulled out a chilled bottle of wine, placing it, a wine key and two long-stemmed glasses on the table in front of Joey. He opened the bottle as Penelope took the seat next to him, fanning her long blonde hair so it could dry in the warm breeze.

"I got some information you wanted," Joey said after he'd filled their glasses.

Penelope took a sip and paused a beat, thinking. "Oh, right. You looked into Emilio's background?"

"Yes, and Emilio Babineau isn't squeaky clean, that's for sure, but he's got no criminal history involving interfering with minors," Joey said, sitting back in his chair and admiring the view. The sun was dipping close to the water and the sky was lit with vibrant orange and pink slashes.

Penelope glanced at him and said, "What did you find?"

"He's got an interesting past," Joey said. "Some drug arrests, mostly minor stuff like marijuana possession. But he did get arrested once for possession of heroin."

Penelope put her glass down on the table and turned to Joey. "Emilio was involved with heroin? When?"

Joey sat forward in his chair and said, "Twenty years ago, roughly. He was a youthful offender for all of his arrests."

Penelope nodded. "He talks about rebuilding his life after a rough childhood in interviews, and he alluded to some trouble in his past, but I never knew any specifics."

"He hasn't been arrested since then, so legally he's clean. Maybe he's just gotten good at not getting caught."

Penelope picked up her wineglass and eased back into her chair. "I'm just having a hard time understanding why he would do the things he did on Friday night. He's smart enough not to drive after he's had too much to drink, but dumb enough to drink with a group of underage kids and then invite them into his house. Why take such a risk?"

"He probably wasn't thinking clearly at the time, Penny," Joey said. "He was drunk. They all were, right?"

"I suppose. That's what I've heard anyway," Penelope said. "But I still feel like he couldn't have done what they're saying. I can't picture him leaving two incapacitated girls by themselves without trying to help them. Then the next minute I think maybe he could have, especially when I think about the things Summer said. I got the feeling she hates him."

"If what she says is true, that's not surprising. And clearly Emilio has a temper, which we've all seen, and maybe she saw up close, if they were involved."

"I suppose," Penelope said.

"Let's just say, maybe he drove the girls back to town and they got into an argument about something and he just left them behind and went home. If he was drunk it's possible he didn't realize how bad off the girls were," Joey suggested.

"I don't know. I guess that's possible, but why would he lock them inside his own building?" Penelope asked. "He had to realize when they were found the police would come directly to him." Penelope thought for a minute. "Who else would have left them in there? Shane has a key, but he has nothing to gain and everything to lose in all of this. He's the main investor in the restaurant and having Emilio, his celebrity chef, behind bars can't be good for business."

Joey nodded and said, "Yeah, I thought about why Shane might want Emilio out of the picture. Do you think he'd go through all of this to get a shot at his wife?"

"Dominique?" Penelope asked, lightly rubbing her chin with her finger. "It seems like a lot to go through just to make a pass at someone's wife. She's gorgeous, but Shane is a rich and powerful guy. Wouldn't there be an easier way to do it?"

"I don't know, think about it. If Emilio gets locked up, for ten years at least, that clears the way for Shane to make his move on her. Prison is hard on a marriage. I can't imagine Dominique would be too thrilled with Emilio if he gets put away for his association with two underage girls."

"Well, when you put it that way it sounds more plausible," Penelope said, pouring herself some more wine. "Shane's a jerk but I still can't believe he would risk his career to frame Emilio."

"You'd be surprised what some people will do to get what they want, Penny, especially people like him, ones who are used to never hearing the word 'no.'"

"So, if you were investigating this case, what would you be doing?" Penelope asked.

Joey thought for a moment and said, "If I were convinced, as you are, of Emilio's innocence—"

"I'm not *convinced*," Penelope interrupted. "I'm just leaning towards him being innocent based on my history with him and how he feels about his wife. I can't see him blowing up his whole life in one drunken evening. Everything seemed to be going great for him until Friday night."

"Right, okay, you're not convinced; you've got a gut feeling he isn't our guy. So, if it were my case, I'd look to see who benefits from Emilio going down. And from my experience, you can count on it either being personal, financial or part of a bigger crime that we don't know about. If you feel he's innocent and that he's being framed, you need to find out who gains the most from Emilio being out of the picture," Joey said, topping off his own glass.

Penelope stared at the sunset, lost in thought. "I can't think of anyone besides Shane, and I don't even think that makes sense."

"Emilio's a businessman in a competitive industry. Maybe he's got enemies who don't want to see him become successful. The guy's a hothead. I'm sure he's ticked off his fair share of people over the years," Joey said.

"I can see that," Penelope said. "Emilio's never been one to bottle up his emotions. But I always thought that was part of his whole persona. You know, poor kid comes up out of nowhere, lives the rock and roll lifestyle, then cleans up and makes it big in the culinary world."

"That's a good story," Joey said. "It will be interesting to see how the rest of his story plays out."

"You know, he mentioned not everyone was behind him bringing his restaurant chain to the island. After all the trouble Shane went through to get permission to film here, I figured he was going through some of the same issues with the locals. Maybe someone is trying to stop the restaurant from being built and getting rid of Emilio at the same time."

Joey sat forward in his chair and nodded. "You might have something there, Penny Blue. Did Emilio ever mention specifics to you about the restaurant? Anyone in particular very vocal about not wanting a Craw Daddy's location on Andrea Island?"

"Not that he said. I haven't heard anyone complaining about it. I'll ask Jeanne when I see her if she knows any gossip."

Joey's phone pinged in his pocket and he pulled it out. He read the screen and smiled, turning it around to show Penelope.

She read the text, "You owe me one, partner. Christine Amato, Brattleboro, VT. Amato's Farmers Market."

"Looks like my partner tracked down your old classmate," Joey said. "Want to give her a call?"

Penelope nodded, already reaching for her phone. She pulled open the business's page and dialed the number. It rang a few times and then a woman answered. "Amato's."

"Could I speak with Christine, please?" Penelope asked.

"Speaking," the woman said sweetly.

"Christine, it's Penelope Sutherland," Penelope said hopefully.

The woman hesitated a few seconds and said, "Who?"

"Penelope Sutherland...we were students together in culinary school."

"Oh, I'm sorry, I didn't put that together right away...what can I do for you?"

Christine sounded distracted, and Penelope didn't think she remembered exactly who she was.

"I'm calling about Emilio Babineau. We're working together now," Penelope said. She anticipated Christine's reaction, hoping the woman wouldn't hang up on her or rush her off the phone.

"Emilio Babineau," Christine said warily, lowering her voice.

"Yes, and, well, it's kind of a sensitive topic. We're opening a new restaurant and I'm his consulting chef...some issues from his past have been brought up by the investors and the local press. Frankly, we're trying to head off any negative buzz before opening. I was wondering if you could help us out, shed some light on what happened back when we were all in school together." Penelope raised her eyebrows and shrugged her shoulders at Joey, who gave her a thumbs up from across the table.

Penelope could hear the woman pull the phone away from her ear and speak to someone in the background. She came back on the line and said, "I don't think I can, we're busy now and—"

"Please, we're getting close to launching the new place in Florida, and our financing might be in jeopardy. I just wanted to see—"

"Are you really working with Emilio?" the woman cut in, the wariness in her voice increasing.

"Yes, and I'm sorry to bring it up, but I remembered you were involved in an incident with him, back in school, and I wanted to see if anyone had come around asking you anything about him."

"No, I haven't been in touch with anyone. To be honest, I haven't thought about school for a long time, or talked with anyone from back then either, until now. You don't have to worry about me saying anything. I wish you all the luck with your new venture. So if you'll excuse me..."

"Wait, Christine, can you tell me what happened between you and Emilio in your own words? Just so I know what we're up against in case it comes out?"

Christine hesitated a few moments then said, "Let me call you back on my cell phone. I'm at the front register and I don't want to be overheard."

A few minutes later Penelope's phone rang and she snatched it up, walking out to the balcony.

"I remember you now, Penelope. Emilio always talked about how much potential you had in the kitchen."

"Thanks...he always encouraged me, all of us, as I remember. So, you moved to Vermont?"

"Yeah, my husband's family is here. We own a small farm and an attached general store, us and his parents. We've got two little ones, another on the way," Christine said, a small laugh in her tone.

"Congratulations," Penelope said.

"We're happy. Busy. Vermont is so peaceful...I was never one for the hustle of the city," Christine said, her tone light and airy. "We got married right out of school...my husband is a chef too, self-taught, restaurant. Not from the institute. We do some catering on the side once in a while, so I keep my hand in the kitchen when I'm not busy with the kids."

"You got married right out of school? So not long after everything happened with Emilio," Penelope said, veering the conversation back to the matter at hand.

Christine faltered a minute and said, "Yes, it was soon after he left, after we all graduated."

"Can you tell me what exactly happened?" Penelope asked gently.

"It was such a mess." Christine sighed. "I wouldn't want what happened then to derail his work now. He was so wonderful to be around. I'd never had anyone pay so much attention to me before...I was naïve and I took that attention the wrong way, and I fell in love with him. Luckily for me, he never acted on it, even though I threw myself at him once after a few of us went out to dinner. I managed to get him alone, I'd had two glasses of wine, for the first time in my life, and I went to kiss him...he pushed me away, gently, and drove me home. He never mentioned it again, but it was hard for me to be around him after that, I was so embarrassed."

"So you never had an intimate relationship with Emilio?"

"No. And I initiated the one encounter we had, not him. I feel terrible about everything that happened afterwards."

"I talked to Summer Farrington too...she told a very different story about things that happened between her and Emilio," Penelope said. She pressed the phone closer to hear ear to hear over the wind on the other end, Christine obviously outside while she talked. She pictured her walking through the fields of her farm.

"Yes, well, she would," Christine said grimly. "I was so upset when I got back to the dorm that night, just humiliated from embarrassment. She was in the common room studying. She put two and two together when I told her a bunch of us had been out with Emilio. Between the wine and just needing to get it off my chest, I just told her that I'd made a move on him."

"So after hearing your story, she went out with Emilio too? Did she initiate a relationship with him?"

"No, as far as I know, they were never alone together. Except maybe in the kitchen. She made up the whole story, took what happened to me and wove her own tale, hoping to get something out of him. Money, I guess."

"What are you saying?" Penelope asked, trying to make sense of everything.

"Summer is a nice girl, but she's got a ruthless side. I caught her skimming tips during student services one night. She offered to cut me in to keep quiet. I'm ashamed to say I took the money. She did it all the time, and whenever we worked together she'd slip me a wad of bills at the end of the night."

All the culinary students at the institute were required to work a daily shift waiting tables at one of the fine dining restaurants sponsored by the school. They learned front of the house skills and also earned tips for spending money. Tips were supposed to be split evenly among everyone on the wait staff working the floor. Holding back tips was against school policy, and could result in a reprimand, or worse, from the dean. Penelope could hear the shame in Christine's voice. If she felt bad about something relatively minor like skimming tips all these years later, she couldn't imagine the guilt she must be feeling about the role she played in getting Emilio fired from the institute.

"I've never really gotten over everything that happened...I didn't tell the whole truth about Emilio. I lied, actually. I was too afraid to go up against Summer. She threatened to tell the dean about the tip money...at the time that seemed like such a big deal, the possibility of getting expelled for a few extra dollars."

"Sounds like Summer manipulated you," Penelope said cautiously. "Doesn't seem like what happened is your fault."

"Well," Christine said, sighing, "the one thing I can say for myself is I never lied about Emilio directly to the dean. But at that point I'd done enough damage. She used what I told her about Emilio to make her complaint seem more valid, I guess. I ruined his teaching career in one night by confiding in the wrong person. She ran with her own version of the story, and ran him out of town."

Penelope shook her head sadly, starring out at the ocean. After a few seconds she said, "So let me get it right. You made a pass at Emilio, which he refused, told Summer about it, and she concocted a story about sleeping with him to further her career?"

"And to squeeze money out of him and the school. That's it in a nutshell. She's on her way to the top...chef de cuisine in Manhattan already, and I heard she's auditioning for some of those chef competition shows. You haven't heard the last of Summer Farrington, not by a long shot."

"I'm really sorry for all that you went through, Christine. I wish we'd been better friends back in school. Maybe I could have helped," Penelope said.

"Well, hopefully me telling you will help him now," Christine said, her voice trailing off. "If it does, it's the least I can do, maybe make up for some of it."

"I hope so too. Thanks for talking with me, Christine," Penelope said. "You've been very helpful."

Christine was silent for a moment and then said, "Can you tell Emilio I'm sorry? I never meant for everything to get so out of control. I was confused and young, missing home."

"I'll be sure to tell him," Penelope said. "Take care of yourself."

Penelope went back inside and related her conversation to Joey.

"Well, now you have two versions of what may have happened back in school," Joey said, finishing his wine.

"I believe Christine's version of events. It fits better with what I know about Emilio."

"These things are hard to call, Penny, like I said before. Without real proof, it's all hearsay, on everyone's behalf."

They sat for a few minutes in silence and then Penelope said, "Are you okay? You seem a little distant this evening."

Joey sighed. "I'm okay. I just started thinking today that maybe I shouldn't have come down here and bothered you while you're working. I know you're busy with your job and your friends."

Penelope looked at him and said, "Joey, I'm glad you're here. I'm sorry today was long and it wasn't the best day for me, but being here with you now makes it all worth it. I just hope you're not going to be too bored while I'm working the rest of the week. You can always come down and visit me on the set, but I'll probably put you to work."

Joey smiled, looking a bit more relaxed. "No, I won't be bored. Are you serious about me coming to cook with you on the set? I make awesome salads."

Penelope stood up from her chair and went over to Joey, sitting down on his lap. She draped her arms loosely around his neck and whispered in his ear, "I've seen your salads. You could use some professional instruction."

Joey snorted laughter. "Oh yeah? What's wrong with my salads?"

Penelope laughed and kissed his ear. She sat up and looked at him in the eyes and said, "You have to watch your proportions. Sometimes there's way too much lettuce and not enough toppings. Or you don't have a big enough variety of dressings. You have to work on making your salads more balanced. And prettier."

Joey shook his head, still laughing. "Okay, I'll come down to the set and you can show me how to make a salad the right way."

"You're on," Penelope said, and kissed him.

CHAPTER 25

Penelope and Joey strolled down the beach towards his cabin. When they passed the marina Penelope turned and said, "I'm going to get my bag off the boat. My laptop is in there and I have to do a few things for work when we get to your place. Do you still have to pick up your suitcase?"

"No, I stopped by earlier and got it," Joey said, squeezing her hand in his.

They walked leisurely down the dock, their hands linked at the fingers. It was dark at the dock; the lantern posts at each slip were old and didn't throw off much light. Suddenly out of the darkness they heard a voice.

"You better watch yourself, poking around in peoples' business. Some folks don't like it when you bring up the past, little lady," a gravelly voice said from the shadows. Penelope and Joey stopped short and turned towards the slip. The two old fishermen were on their dock, one of them smoking a cigar that partially lit his stubble-sheathed chin when he inhaled.

"Excuse me?" Penelope said. "Are you talking to me?"

"No, I'm talking to your boyfriend," the fisherman said. "One of them, anyway." They both snickered laughter, slapping their thighs with hands that weren't holding beer cans.

Joey stiffened next to her and said, "Have a good night, old timer." He tightened his grip on Penelope's hand and pulled her toward the *Isn't She Lovely*.

"Oh, we'll have a good night, all right. You do the same." The sound of their laughter followed Penelope and Joey down the dock.

When they reached the boat, Penelope rolled her eyes at Joey and shrugged her shoulders. "I have no idea what that guy is talking about. Sorry. I swear neither one of them has ever said a word to any of us."

Joey glanced at her, looking annoyed. "They're a couple of old drunks. Forget it. Let's just get your stuff and get out of here."

Penelope picked up the white phone next to the glass doors of the boat and rang for the captain, who came up to let her in.

"I'll wait for you out here," Joey said, stepping back onto the deck.

Penelope entered the salon and headed quickly down the spiral stairs. After she'd retrieved her clothes and laptop and emerged from the boat, she saw Joey was staring towards the old fishermen, their faint conversation and laughter floating on the air towards them.

"You okay?" Penelope asked.

"Yeah," Joey said, snapping back to focus. "You ready?"

"I am," Penelope said, holding up her overnight bag. Joey took it from her and slung it over his shoulder and they walked back towards the beach.

When they passed by the old men they fell silent, snickering under their breath. Suddenly one of them said, "There they go, Wainright. I tell you, I will never understand girls. Just as mean to each other as anyone can be."

Penelope stopped abruptly and turned towards the fishermen. She took a step closer and squinted at them in the dark, digging in her memory for where she'd heard the name. "Wainright...were you a teacher back in the sixties?"

The fisherman beamed, revealing a row of clean white teeth. His friend laughed too, but his dental habits must have been lacking because he had a few open spots on the top row. "Yes, I was...taught English and History for twenty years over there." He waved in the general direction of the school complex.

"I saw your picture in a yearbook over at the Inn," Penelope said.

Mr. Wainright laughed, rocking back and forth in his ancient deck chair.

"Yep, Betty Jeanne was always the sentimental one, hanging on to our history for us."

"Betty Jeanne?" Penelope asked. "Jeanne is Elizabeth Haverford? I thought that was an older sister or something."

"Nope, that's Betty Jeanne. She goes by Jeanne now, of course; it's much more elegant. Jeanne does worry about being elegant. She used to say Betty Jeanne made her sound like she should be slinging beers in a bar in Texas. I always thought it had a nice ring, in a country music kind of way," Mr. Wainright said. "Well, now I guess I know what she meant." He snickered along with his fishing partner.

"So you guys, what? Decided to retire together to this dock? Spend the rest of your days drunk out in the sun?" Joey asked, still sounding annoyed.

"Yeah, son. What's it to you?" the other man asked, spraying hoarse laughter.

"Mr. Wainright," Penelope said, "you knew Jeanne and Rose and Josephine in high school, right?"

"And Henny, yes," he said, nodding agreeably.

"And they were all friends?" Penelope asked.

"Yes. Best friends," he replied. "Until they graduated."

"Penny, let's get out of here," Joey said, grabbing her hand. "It's getting late."

Penelope pulled her hand away from Joey and said, "What happened after graduation? They weren't friends anymore?"

"It's hard to be best friends your whole life. Especially girls like that," Mr. Wainright said cryptically.

"What do you mean, girls like that?" Penelope asked.

"The popular ones. Something always comes along to break them up. I've seen it a hundred times. There was this one group of girls, back in '73..."

His voice trailed off in Penelope's ear and she noticed Joey had started walking away from her towards the shore. She turned and followed him away from the drunk old men.

CHAPTER 26

"Let's stop at Sackler's on the way. I want to get some eggs for the morning," Joey said. His mood had lightened since they'd left the dock.

They arrived at Sackler's right before closing. Bradley was up front, restocking candy in the checkout aisle. Joey headed to the dairy section while Penelope waited for him at the register.

"Hey, Bradley," Penelope said.

He looked up at her and said, "Hi, Miss Sutherland." His eyes were red and his shoulders slumped under his Sackler's Market t-shirt.

"Are you okay?" she asked.

Bradley shrugged his shoulders and murmured, "Not really."

"What's going on?" Penelope asked, taking a step towards him.

Bradley hesitated, then told her in a rush, "Sabena Lambert died today. We were friends."

"Bradley, I'm so sorry," Penelope said. "I knew her too."

Bradley nodded, sighing gruffly. "I wish I could have done something to help her."

"How well did you know her?" Penelope asked, then

suddenly something snapped into place for her. "Bradley, was she your girlfriend?"

Bradley's eyes snapped up to hers quickly and the word "No" died on his lips. Then he began to nod, and he turned away from Penelope.

She placed a hand on his shoulder and felt it stiffen beneath his t-shirt. "I saw part of your baseball jersey in her room, along with some ripped-up pictures," Penelope said gently.

Bradley nodded and regained some composure. "We dated in secret. My mom knew from the start, but Sabena wasn't allowed." He pulled out his phone and scrolled through some pictures, stepping closer to Penelope so they could both see.

"Stop," Penelope said. "Go back one?"

Bradley scrolled back and Penelope saw the whole image of the beach picture she'd seen in the box. In this version Bradley sat next to Sabena, and it was his finger underneath her bathing suit strap. "I saw that one in her room."

Bradley continued to thumb through the pictures, some of him in uniform, lots of them at school or on the beach together. "I loved her. But we broke up."

Penelope looked at the side of his face and saw genuine anguish in his expression. "What happened?" she asked quietly.

"I got the scholarship. I'm going to be so far away, really soon. Bean had two more years of high school...my mom didn't think it was fair to keep her from dating other people that whole time. And she said I'd want to see other people too. But..." He broke off, confused. "Bean didn't want to go to college. She was staying here. That doesn't fit in with my plans. She flipped out on me when I sent in my acceptance."

"I saw some college entrance information in her room," Penelope said hesitantly.

Bradley looked at her with surprise. "News to me," he said

with a touch of bitterness. "She always said she wouldn't leave her mom all alone on the island like everyone else did."

"I can't imagine someone at that age realizes how big that kind of decision is. Do you know how her mom felt about it?"

Bradley shook his head quickly. "Oh no, we weren't allowed to act like we knew each other around her mom. They live in a different reality from the rest of us over there."

"Penelope, I was thinking about you today," Henny said, walking up quickly from the back of the store. Bradley tucked his phone back into his pocket. "Do you want me to make another shrimp order for you?"

"Yes, thank you. I almost forgot. Today was crazy. Henny," Penelope said, "have you heard of anyone not being happy about the new restaurant?"

Henny thought for a moment and said, "No, but I have heard some grumbling about the new chef in town. I heard he wants to import all his seafood down in New Orleans, something about maintaining the authentic local flavor of his restaurants."

"Really," Penelope said. "How do the fishermen feel about that?"

Henny put her fists on her hips over her apron strings. "They don't like it one bit. They were thinking they were going to get all this extra business. Well, maybe they will after all. This Babineau character might just realize after a while it makes more sense to source his ingredients locally."

"I'm sure if you talked to him he'd understand. I can't imagine he'd want to deal with all of those long-distance shipments," Penelope said.

"Exactly. And things around here have a way of not working out for people who don't stick to the island rules," Henny said, lowering her voice.

Bradley ducked away towards the back of the store. Joey

wandered up with a basket full of groceries. They paid and said goodbye, Henny locking the door behind them.

As they walked in the dark to the cabin Penelope said, "Bradley and Sabena were dating but they broke up when he got a scholarship to college," Penelope said.

"That's a shame. He must be feeling terrible about her passing away," Joey said.

"I know. That's a big burden of guilt to be carrying around at his age."

"He didn't cause what happened, Penny," Joey said.

"True. But I'm sure that doesn't make what happened any easier for him to deal with."

CHAPTER 27

The next morning on the set, Penelope and her crew sped through breakfast and were cleaning up in preparation for lunch when Shane came down to talk to Penelope.

"Penelope, I'm sorry I acted like such an ass yesterday," Shane said, his blue eyes peering out from under his baseball cap. "You're not easily replaceable like I said you were. You're a valuable asset to our team. I appreciate everything you do for everyone. Okay? So, I'm sorry."

Penelope folded her arms across her chest and said, "Okay, thank you. Apology accepted."

Shane turned on his heel and started to walk away.

"Shane, wait," Penelope said.

"What?" he asked testily, turning back around.

"It's none of my business, but—"

"If you have to start by saying that, then you might want to reconsider the next thing you say to me," Shane warned.

"But," Penelope said, pressing forward, "you're putting your relationship with Emilio in jeopardy with the attention you're paying to his wife."

Shane snorted a laugh. "You're right. It is none of your business."

"What's going on with you and Dominique? I know that's

why Emilio attacked you up on the roof. You're getting too close."

Shane took a step toward her but Penelope stood her ground. "Nothing is going on with me and Dominique." He stared at her for a second, then looked away before continuing. "She's my business partner's wife. My friend's wife. She asked me to stay over, and I did, thinking maybe...but she made it clear after I was there, it was only for security out at the house. It was a mistake not telling Emilio about it."

"Trust is a hard thing to regain once it's lost. In order to keep your business relationship going, not to mention your friendship with Emilio, you should back off of Dominique. Think about how things look to him...he loves her," Penelope said quietly.

Shane sighed and said, "I know. Not that I need to explain myself, especially to you, but I do understand that. It's not a mistake I plan on making again."

Shane went back inside the Inn without another word. After a few minutes, Penelope followed him to check on Arlena and see what she might like for lunch. On her way through the hallway she looked in and saw a few members of the crew setting up lights and microphones in the library, getting ready for another day of filming the party scene. She glanced at the bookshelves and saw they had kept most of Jeanne's books in place, removing some of the more obvious covers and obscuring some of the shelves with vases and other items.

"It's quite something, isn't it?" Jeanne said, startling Penelope.

"Oh, Jeanne," Penelope said. "I didn't see you there." Penelope looked down and saw they'd propped the picture of Jeanne and Robert on the floor just outside the door. Jeanne bent to pick it up.

"I'll just take this upstairs until they're finished using the library," Jeanne said, heading for the stairs.

"Jeanne," Penelope said, following her. "Your name is Elizabeth Haverford?"

"Why, yes, dear," Jeanne said, smiling.

"I saw your name on the bill of sale of Emilio's restaurant. You owned that building?" Penelope asked. One of the grips walked down the stairs, cords draped over his shoulders, his heavy boots thumping on the old stairs.

"Oh, yes, that was originally my uncle's hardware store. He didn't have children of his own so he left it to me when he died. We've leased it out for different businesses over the years, but it's been vacant now for at least five. Then Shane came along and offered to buy it, for himself and that Emilio fellow from New Orleans," Jeanne said.

"Hey, Boss, you want us to get started on the chicken breasts?" Quentin stuck his head in the front door and called to her.

She turned around and said, "Yes, go ahead. But only just prep it up. Nothing gets fired until we see the whites of their eyes." She turned back to Jeanne. "You didn't change your name to Daniels when you married your husband?"

Jeanne's smile faltered for a second and she said, "I did, but then I changed it back. It was too painful."

"Penelope," Arlena called from the top of the staircase. "Gavin and I will have lunch upstairs with Sienna and Max in your room again, if that's okay."

"Sure, Arlena, I'll send it up when we break," Penelope said.

Jeanne turned to head up the stairs after another pair of crew members hurried past. Penelope watched her go, lost in thought.

*   *   *

After lunch service was through, Penelope said to her chefs, "Guys, go ahead and get everything cleared down and then you can go for the day. They're not going to need us again. Maybe you can get an hour or two on the beach before sunset."

Her crew worked quickly to get everything put away, cleared down and locked up, then happily headed for the cabin they were sharing to get changed for the beach. Penelope did a quick walkthrough to be sure everything was in place and then went to her room to change also. Pulling on a short sundress and sandals, Penelope took a walk down Ocean Avenue. She decided to stop at Rose's to get a bottle of water on the way.

Rose's door was pulled closed and her little handwritten sign that said she'd be back in ten minutes was taped to the glass. Penelope sat down on the bench and waited, pulling her backpack onto her lap so she could lean against the splintering wood. She looked at the front glass of Rose's, watching the reflection of a few people walking down the sidewalk on the other side of the street. The glass seemed bowed, giving the effect of a panoramic lens like the view from inside a fishbowl.

When Penelope didn't see Rose return after a few minutes, she got up from the bench to see if her old yellow Volvo was parked in the gravel lot. Moving around to the side of the building, Penelope saw it parked there as usual, backed into the last spot by the entrance to the apartment. The trunk was open and the windows of the car were rolled down. The screen door to the apartment entrance had come unlatched and was banging open against the wall of the building.

"Rose?" Penelope called. She went to the doorway and caught the thin aluminum door as it blew open again. "Rose? Are you up there?" She peered into the dark foyer and up the stairs but couldn't see anyone. She closed the screen door and surveyed the trunk, seeing a few grocery bags from Sackler's leaning together towards the rear of the car.

She grabbed the bags and pulled the screen door open again, climbing the stairs up to Rose's apartment.

"Rose?" Penelope called again as she climbed the creaking stairs.

"Who is it?" Rose called sharply from behind her apartment door on the landing.

"It's me, Penelope. I've brought up your groceries."

Rose opened the door quickly and looked at Penelope, then down to her hands where she held the grocery bags. She stepped outside of the apartment and said, "You didn't have to do that, hon. I was heading back down for them."

"It's no problem," Penelope said. "Happy to help."

Rose stepped forward and took the bags from her. "Thank you." She stood in front of her closed door, staying silent. Penelope took a step back onto the landing and turned towards the stairs.

"Did you need something from the shop? I'll be down in a few minutes after I get these things put away," Rose called after her after she made her way halfway down the steps.

Penelope glanced back over her shoulder, her hand on the slick wooden railing. "No, that's okay. I was going to get some water but it's not important. Do you want me to close the trunk of your car?"

"Oh, yes, that would be great. Thank you, Penelope," Rose said, backing into her apartment with her groceries.

Penelope went back out into the bright sunlight and squinted, her eyes having adjusted to the dark interior of Rose's stairway. She walked over to the rear of Rose's car and swung the trunk down. It gave out a groan of protest as it went.

Penelope pressed on it again to be sure it had latched, bouncing the car slightly on its wheels. She walked around the side of the car and glanced inside. The backseat was littered with napkins and papers. A pair of sunglasses and a beach bag sat on the backseat and a fine coating of sand dusted the floorboards. A flash of glittery bright pink caught her eye and she paused to take another look.

Wedged in the crease of the bench seat was a sparkly pink tube. Penelope looked at it curiously, her heartbeat slowing to a dull thud in her chest. Penelope glanced up at the apartment windows and when she didn't see any movement, gently lifted the rear door handle. Finding it unlocked, Penelope slowly pulled the door open. A loud metallic groan broke the silence and Penelope froze, looking up at the windows again. She quickly grabbed some napkins from the backseat and used them to pull the pink tube from the fold in the seat without touching it with her fingers. After taking another quick look around, she wrapped the tube in the napkins and tucked it into the interior zipper of her backpack.

Penelope eased the car door closed, leaning on it until she heard it click, and after taking another quick look at Rose's windows, walked out of the parking lot.

CHAPTER 28

Penelope walked quickly down Ocean Avenue, pausing for a moment when she came to Emilio's restaurant space. A couple of construction workers wearing hard hats carried boxes of tiles from Emilio's pickup truck around the side of the building, stacking them against the wall in the parking lot. Penelope crossed the street when she saw Emilio leaning against the truck, his phone pulled up to his ear. He ended his call and crossed his arms, staring up at the roof of his building.

"Chef," Penelope said, walking up beside him.

"Penelope," Emilio said. "How are you doing?"

Penelope gripped the straps of her backpack in both hands and said, "Okay. Off early today. I see you got your truck back."

Emilio nodded and said, "Yeah, they went over the whole thing and didn't find any trace of the girls. My lawyer argued that it's a company vehicle, that I'm not the only one with access to it. He did his magic lawyer thing and they released it to me. I still don't know how Rebekkah's purse got back there."

"I might," Penelope said carefully. "I'm not sure yet, but I think someone might be setting you up, trying to get you kicked off the island."

Emilio snorted. "Nice. Well, that alone wouldn't be a big deal, but they're trying to ruin my life in the process. If this all sticks I could go to jail, lose my wife, lose my business...who would do something like that?"

"I'm still working that out," Penelope said. "Chef, I talked to Summer. Christine too. We talked about the complaints they filed back at school."

Emilio eyed her cautiously, then crossed his arms tightly over his chest. "So, you ready to write me off now too?"

"No. Can you tell me exactly what happened?"

"I'm not supposed to say. Like I said before, it's all sealed in the agreement. They shouldn't be talking about me...I could sue them."

"Chef, Summer says you two had had a sexual relationship, and Christine says she just backed Summer's story because they had done some other things together that could've gotten them into trouble with the dean...Who is telling the truth?"

"All I can say is, the witch hunt that happened at the institute is behind me. I got too close to my students, I realize that now, and I paid for it. Literally. I never had a relationship with Summer, romantic or otherwise. If Christine says I did, then...she'll have to live with herself, I guess, but we both know the truth. Look, I've moved on from the mistakes of my past. More than once now."

"Okay, Chef. For what it's worth, I believe you," Penelope said, scuffing the sidewalk with the toe of her sneaker.

Emilio's expression softened and he placed a hand on her shoulder. "That means a lot, Penelope. Thanks."

Penelope said goodbye and told him she'd be in touch. She walked north up the avenue heading towards Joey's cabin, turning over everything in her mind. When she got to Josie's she saw Joey sitting out on the deck, drinking a beer and talking with Jonny Daniels.

"Joey, hey." Penelope waved from the sidewalk.

"There she is," Joey said, waving her over. "Come and join me."

Penelope went in through the front door of Josie's. As she headed out to the deck, she noticed a photograph she hadn't seen before. It was a close-up of Rose and Josie, their heads pressed together, their long hair falling in a cascade over their shoulders. They smiled widely at the camera. Penelope thought it looked just like the selfies everyone was taking these days, only this one had to have been taken in the early seventies. Penelope went out to the deck, joining Joey at his table. Jonny gave her a welcoming smile and said, "Beer?"

Penelope nodded and said, "Please."

When Jonny left, she pulled her backpack from her shoulders and opened it, pulling out the pink tube wrapped in napkins and placing it on the table.

"What's that?" Joey asked, eyeing the wad of napkins.

"Lipstick. I found it in Rose's car," Penelope said, nodding at the table.

Joey turned to her and smiled. "You're always bringing me lipstick. What are you saying? Is this one tainted like last time?"

"I don't think so." Penelope carefully unscrewed the cap and pulled the wand from the tube, immediately smelling artificial strawberries. "It's the same lipstick I saw both girls use on Friday night right before I left the beach party. I remember it specifically. Now, how did it get into the back of Rose's car?"

Jonny emerged from the restaurant, two pint glasses in his hands. "Here you go," Jonny said.

"Jonny," Penelope asked, "how does your Aunt Rose feel about Emilio Babineau?"

Jonny's smile faltered and he put his hands on his hips. "I don't know. She's never been a big believer in change."

"So she'd rather not see Craw Daddy's expand onto the

island?" Joey asked, picking up on Penelope's line of thinking.

"I guess not," Jonny said. "She worries about this place suffering from the competition, but I told her it's going to be two completely different places. We're a local old-school destination spot. His will be corporate. It's a chain. What is the appeal of eating in a restaurant that is exactly like a bunch of other restaurants? I told her I don't see how he's going to make it here. There's only so much business to go around."

"So are you worried about your business suffering?" Penelope asked.

"Well, sure, but I think we're going to do just fine. Rose says we're making more money this season than the past three years put together. Mostly because of you guys, which we appreciate."

"Wait, Rose does your books?" Penelope asked.

Jonny laughed, turning when he noticed a couple enter the restaurant and head to the bar. "Yeah, we're partners in the restaurant and she does the books. So, are you guys okay? I've got to get behind the bar."

"Yeah, thanks, man," Joey said.

After he left Penelope pulled out her phone to make a call, scrolling through her recently dialed numbers and selecting one. She put the phone up to her ear and said, "Finish your beer. It's almost time for the Happiest Hour."

CHAPTER 29

Joey and Penelope walked back towards the Inn. When they passed Rose's beach shop Penelope noticed the door was closed, but there was no note on the window about when Rose would return. She quickened her step and urged Joey to walk faster.

The parking lot of the Inn was quiet and it looked like Shane had called an end to the day. The usual hustle and bustle of the busy film crew had given way to a quiet late afternoon. Penelope figured most of them were out on the beach or at the pool. When they entered, Penelope ducked her head into the library and saw that it was empty. Cables and cords were snaked around the corners and a large light tripod stood by the windows. Penelope pulled Joey's hand and they peered into the restaurant, but it was empty too, except for a few of the sound guys who were sitting around one of the dining tables having a meeting.

"Hey, guys," Penelope said, looking around the room. "When did we wrap for the day?"

"About a half hour ago," one of the sound techs said, his large earphones still draped around his neck.

"Okay, thanks," Penelope said. She glanced at the clock on the wall and saw it was a little after three thirty. "Jeanne must be up on the roof, getting ready," she said to Joey.

They made their way upstairs, taking the steps quickly all the way to the top. When Penelope opened the door into the bright sunshine, she was out of breath.

Joey wiped his brow and said, "You really wanted to get to happy hour, huh?"

Penelope walked out onto the deck and looked towards the bar, which stood empty. "No one is up here yet," she said to Joey, pausing to think. "Maybe she's down in the kitchen."

"Wait. Look over there," Joey said.

Penelope turned to look and didn't see anyone at first, but when she got closer she saw Jeanne's back. She was standing by the railing next to the canopy, staring out at the ocean. As Penelope approached, she saw that Jeanne appeared to be talking to herself, but she couldn't make out what she was saying.

"Jeanne?" Penelope called, moving closer.

"Penelope, dear," Jeanne said, without turning around. "You're too early. We're not quite ready yet. Would you be a dear and give us a few more minutes?"

"Sure...um," Penelope said, looking back at Joey and shrugging. "Are you okay?"

Jeanne continued to stare out at the ocean and said, "Yes, yes, we're okay."

"We?" Penelope asked. Joey moved behind Penelope and put his hand on her arm, stopping her from getting closer to Jeanne.

Jeanne's shoulders shook and she quickly said, "Me, me. I'm fine. Go on, dear. Don't worry, I'm okay."

"Can you turn around and look at me for a second?" Penelope asked. Her skin had gone cold even though the sun was beating down on her and it had to be over ninety degrees on the roof.

"No, no, I can't," Jeanne said. She glanced quickly towards the canopy, its black fabric blowing lazily in the wind.

Penelope took another step closer to Jeanne, Joey's body tensing by her side. She saw his hand go to the spot on his belt where he usually kept his gun. Penelope could see the silhouette of someone behind the black fabric that hung down from the canopy.

"Whoever is back there, come out now," Joey said.

A short gray nose of a gun poked out from behind the fabric, pointed directly at Jeanne. Penelope's knees buckled slightly when she saw the deeply wrinkled suntanned hand that was holding it.

"Come out from behind there," Joey said. "And put the gun down."

Rose emerged from the corner, still holding the gun, aiming it at Jeanne.

"Okay, I'm going to need you to put the gun down and step away from it," Joey demanded.

"You don't have any authority here, Detective. You're a guest on this island...an outsider. Where do you get off telling me what to do?"

Rose's hand shook slightly but she seemed pretty sure of her grip on the gun.

"Rose, what are you doing?" Penelope pleaded. "Jeanne is your friend...you guys have been friends for over forty years."

"Ha, friends, that's rich," Rose said. "Who could be friends with someone like her?" Rose waved at Jeanne with the gun, a disgusted look on her face.

"Rose, you have to stop this now," Jeanne said, her voice shaking. "You don't know what you're talking about."

"Oh, I don't know what I'm talking about?" Rose laughed. "I know everything...don't you forget that. I know what you did and I know what you're trying to do. But this time I'm going to put a stop to it. Betty Jeanne isn't going to win."

"Win?" Jeanne said, turning and looking at Rose. "What do you mean, win? I haven't won anything...only a life of heartbreak and disappointment and loss." She looked down at the gun, which was leveled at her birdlike chest.

"Betty Jeanne always gets her way," Rose said to Penelope. "That's how it's always been. Spoiled little rich girl, but that wasn't enough for her. She had to win at everything, take anything she wanted. And now she's trying to sell out our island right out from under us."

Jeanne's voice remained quiet but quivered with emotion. "You don't know what you're talking about."

"Oh, yes, I do," Rose said. "You brought that drug addict over here, sold him your uncle's store and look what happens. Another innocent girl is dead because of you! Just like when we were younger. You only think about yourself."

"What do you mean *another* girl is dead?" Penelope asked.

Rose spoke to her but kept her gaze on Jeanne. "Betty Jeanne here fell in love with Josie's husband. She had no problem stepping into her dead friend's shoes and marrying him before she was even cold in the ground."

Jeanne looked out at the ocean and then back at Rose. "Josie chose to take her own life. She was very depressed after little Jonny was born. I had nothing to do with that."

Rose snorted. "But you did! You were right here when she fell off the roof. You could have stopped her."

"How would you know, you weren't here!" Jeanne yelled. Penelope jumped, surprised at the normally placid Jeanne showing her anger.

"I know you. I know if you had wanted to, you could have stopped her from going over. But you wanted her to die so you could have her husband. You probably even encouraged her to jump. Did you give her a boost up onto the railing?"

"Shut up," Jeanne said. "You're a miserable person and you always have been. Sneaking around, lying about everything, causing trouble. You thought Josie was your best friend, but she didn't trust you as far as she could throw you."

Rose stepped closer, tightening her grip on the gun. "I loved Josie like a sister and you just watched her die. You're finally going to pay for that. We're going to watch you fall just like you watched Josie fall. Get up on that railing," she demanded, waving the gun at Jeanne.

"Rose, give me the gun," Joey said. "You don't want to do this."

"But I do," Rose sneered. "I've wanted to do this for forty years."

Rose took a step closer towards Jeanne and began to squeeze the trigger.

"No!" Penelope yelled loudly. Joey lunged for Rose, grabbing her thin wrist and aiming the gun into the air just as she pulled the trigger. A single gunshot sounded and Penelope could hear shouts from the pool area below.

Joey gripped Rose's wrist tightly with one hand and pulled the gun from her grip with the other.

"You're hurting me," Rose spat at him. He handed the gun to Penelope. She couldn't believe how heavy it was in her hand, and warm to the touch. She stared at it in shock, realizing she had never held a gun before in her life.

"Police! Drop your weapon," a woman's voice said from behind them. Detective Torres came out onto the patio, her gun drawn and her arms rigid.

Joey stood behind Rose, pinning her arms behind her back. Jeanne was leaning against the wall of the patio, one hand over her heart, and Penelope stood frozen, still looking at the gun in her hand.

"Ma'am, put the gun down," Detective Torres said loudly.

Penelope snapped back to the present and laid the gun carefully down on a nearby table. Detective Torres walked over to the table and picked up the gun, tucking it in her waistband at the small of her back.

"What's going on up here?" she asked, relaxing slightly. "I heard a gunshot."

CHAPTER 30

Jeanne, Joey and Penelope followed Detective Torres down the stairs as she escorted a handcuffed Rose to the door of the Inn. When they reached the landing, they noticed a crowd gathering on the main floor. Most of the cast and crew who were staying at the Inn had come in from the pool or out of their rooms to see what was happening. Emilio was in the foyer talking with Shane, and all four of Penelope's chefs and Regan stood together in the doorway of the library, still wearing their chef coats. Everyone was milling around with looks of concern on their faces.

"Aunt Rose!" Regan called to her. "What's going on?"

"Regan, what are you doing here? You know you're not allowed to be at the Inn," Rose said.

Regan looked at her, a confused expression on his face. "What do you mean? I'm not a little kid anymore. You can't forbid me from going places."

"You shouldn't be in this building. It's disrespectful to your grandmother," Rose said. She tried to tug her hands away from Detective Torres but she held on to Rose tighter. "You know, just because she isn't here to tell you what to do doesn't mean you can just do whatever you please."

"Aunt Rose, what are you talking about?" Regan asked.

"I know you think you're all grown up, but you're not. I saw you, you know, the other night when you were with that drug addict chef," she glared at Emilio, "and those two stupid girls, stumbling around drunk as can be. I followed you to make sure you wouldn't get caught, driving around drunk like a damn fool."

"I wasn't drunk, Aunt Rose," Regan said. "Wait, you followed me?"

"Yes, I did. I made a promise to your grandmother I would always look out for your father and now I have to look out for you too. And it's a good thing I did. You're already making stupid choices." Rose eyed him up and down.

"Aunt Rose, if you were following us, then you must have seen what happened to Rebekkah and Sabena. Wait, did you see me leave?" Regan asked.

"Yes, I saw you leave," Rose said. "And then I saw those two silly girls come stumbling out of his house and call after you. They were so drunk they thought they could run and catch up to your car. I pulled up to them and offered them a ride back to town."

"I found their lipstick in the backseat of your car today," Penelope said. "And I called Detective Torres to let her know."

"I saw you poking around in my car. That's when I decided to come here and finally settle the score with Betty Jeanne," Rose said. "That and seeing that they've started working on that restaurant even after everything I've done to stop it from opening."

Detective Torres listened with interest and turned to look at Emilio. "What happened to the girls after you picked them up?" she demanded, looking back at Rose.

Rose smirked and looked around the room at the crowd that had gathered. "You are all so stupid. Those girls got in my backseat and were laughing and crying and making no sense at all. They kept whining over and over again that they didn't want to go home and get in trouble with their parents. I didn't think they'd even remember being in my car at all, so I thought I could use them to get rid of you." She glared at Emilio again. "I told them that they should go inside that empty building and rest for a while and sober up before heading home. I took their phones, turned them off and locked the door."

"Why didn't you think to let them out of there the next day?" Detective Torres asked.

Rose shrugged her shoulders and said, "And let everyone know it was me who locked them in there? I don't think so." She laughed and looked at Emilio. "He was always in and out of there. I knew he'd come and find them eventually. And then I'd call the police while he was inside and get him arrested and thrown off the island."

"Unbelievable," Emilio snorted. He turned to Shane and said, "You've brought me onto an island full of crazy people."

Shane shrugged and looked at him incredulously. "It's Rose from the beach shop! I've known her my whole life!"

"Rose," Penelope asked, "how did you get the padlock open to let them inside?"

Rose sniffed, "That was easy. The town manager always leaves his keys lying around. And he's got a set for each of the cabins. I ask him if I can borrow his keys to make duplicates all the time. He never thinks anything of it. I just had to slip off the padlock key, make a copy and return it. It's not like he opens the padlock regularly. I could have kept it for days."

"But how did the girls OD? They were just drunk when I dropped them off at Emilio's. I heard them say something about taking a pharm, but that wouldn't do it, would it?" Regan asked, looking at Joey.

"It depends on what they took," Joey said, looking at

Detective Torres. "It does seem odd that they blacked out around the same time. They must have been on something else."

"Heroin," Rose said, laughing again.

"Excuse me?" Detective Torres said, looking at Rose.

"They smoked heroin. I laced some cigarettes with it and asked them to leave the pack behind inside his restaurant," Rose said smiling. "I thought if the police found heroin on his property, a known drug addict, they would arrest him and kick him out of here. The blonde one bummed a cigarette off of me in the car. I could tell she wasn't a smoker, but I gave her the pack and told her to leave them inside for Emilio."

"Aunt Rose, where did you get heroin?" Regan asked in disbelief.

"Some musician friends of your dad's rented a cabin a while back and left some of their stash behind," Rose said, shrugging. "I threw it in the drawer with all of the other things I've found over the years. You never know when something will come in handy."

"So you locked two inebriated minors behind a padlocked door with no other way out of the building and gave them cigarettes laced with heroin, is that correct?" Detective Torres asked.

"And then I drove back to his house and threw that girl's purse in the back of his truck," Rose said, smiling smugly at Emilio. "Idiot left the back cab unlocked."

"Rose, you've gone completely crazy," Jeanne said, shaking her head sadly at her old friend.

"I'm not crazy," Rose said. "I know exactly what I'm doing. No jury in the world will convict me for just trying to protect my home from people like him. Go ahead and let them try."

CHAPTER 31

A few days later, Penelope knocked on Mrs. Lambert's faded door, squaring her shoulders and taking a deep breath when she heard movement on the other side. When the door opened she was a little surprised to see Mrs. Flores and not Sabena's mom on the other side.

"Mrs. Flores, I hope I'm not intruding," Penelope said, taking a quick glance over the woman's shoulder into the darkened living room behind her.

"No, please, come in," she said kindly.

Penelope stepped inside and offered her a shopping bag. "I brought a few things from the market. Henny made a casserole you can heat up later."

"Thank you," Mrs. Flores said, taking the bag from her. They came through the living room and she said, "Roni, Miss Sutherland is here. She brought some groceries."

Roni Lambert sat in her place on the couch, a blanket pulled around her. Her shoulders caved forward, and her legs were pulled up under her on the couch. She gazed up at Penelope with an expression of calm sadness.

"I know this is an awful time for you—" Penelope began.

"I'm sorry I pushed you the other day," Mrs. Lambert interrupted. "I shouldn't have done that."

Mrs. Flores busied herself in the kitchen, putting the different items Penelope brought away.

"I understand why you did," Penelope said, taking a seat in one of the rattan chairs that flanked the couch, feeling the bamboo-like material give a little under her weight. "What you're going through is the worst thing imaginable."

"Bean is gone, my little girl. I never thought...I just figured we'd always be together," Mrs. Lambert said, tears rolling to the surface. Mrs. Flores hurried from the kitchen and took the seat next to her, wrapping an arm around her shoulders. Mrs. Lambert smiled gratefully at her friend, then said, "I'm so glad Rebekkah woke up."

"She did?" Penelope asked.

"Yes, when I was with her this morning. My husband is there now. I'm heading back over...I was just checking in on Roni, letting her know," Mrs. Flores said.

"That's wonderful news," Penelope said.

"I can't believe Rose did this to us," Mrs. Lambert said suddenly. "I've known her my whole life. How could this have happened here?"

Mrs. Flores hugged her tighter, rocking her gently on the couch. "She's going to get what's coming to her, Roni. We're going to make sure of it."

"Rebekkah might be able to testify to what happened that night," Penelope said hopefully. "Depending on what she remembers. That should help put Rose away for a long time."

"We'll see," Mrs. Flores said. "We're not going to upset her right away. The doctors say that wouldn't be the best thing, the shock of everything all at once. She asked about Sabena first thing after she woke up, how her best friend was. We're waiting to tell her together, when the doctor says it's okay, and when you're ready to go." She squeezed Mrs. Lambert's shoulders again.

Mrs. Lambert brought a tissue up to her nose again, but held in her tears.

After a few seconds of silence, Penelope said, "The production crew wanted to do something to help your families. We feel partly responsible for what happened...It seems that Rose did what she did because we were here on the island."

Mrs. Lambert eyed cautiously her from behind the tissue.

"We took up a collection," Penelope said, reaching into her backpack to pull out two envelopes. "I have one for each of you, actually. I was going to stop by your house on the way back but since you're here..." She reached across and handed Mrs. Flores and Mrs. Lambert the white envelopes, their names visible on the checks through the plastic windows on the front. "Then Shane added to the total after making calls to the executive producers and the studio. We know nothing can make up for the loss of your daughter, and the injury to yours, but the company would like to help if it can." Penelope's mind flipped back to the day before, standing over Shane with her arms crossed while he made the calls after lunch in the tent, then called in the total amounts to payroll to cut the checks for the families.

Mrs. Lambert placed the envelope on the table next to her and sighed. "Is this to get me not to sue you? I'm not going to sign anything."

Penelope shook her head. "No, this is just...from all of us to you. Shane is authorized by the studio to pay funeral and medical costs too. We feel if we can at least take care of that, not that it will be any easier, but having the financial burden lifted might help a little."

Mrs. Flores nodded. "Thank you."

"You're welcome. Sabena and Rebekkah were members of our crew. It's the least we can do," Penelope said, rising from her chair. "I should go. Please tell Rebekkah we miss her, and give her our best wishes...from Shane and everyone else on the set."

Mrs. Flores nodded and rose to show her out. They stopped right before the door when Mrs. Lambert said, "Wait."

Penelope froze, readying herself.

Mrs. Lambert stood up from the couch and went to Penelope, holding out her hand. Penelope took it and shook it gently. "Thanks for everything you did, to help figure out what happened to Bean." She turned to Mrs. Flores and said, "Let's get to the hospital."

When Penelope stepped out onto the porch after saying her goodbyes, her phone pinged in her backpack. She pulled it out and saw she had a text message from Summer Farrington. "Good to hear from you, Penelope. I've still got that job open if you're interested. Stop by the restaurant next time you're in the city."

Penelope read the text again, clicked her screen to dark, and threw her phone back in her bag.

CHAPTER 32

"I guess I'll see you back in New Jersey in a couple of months," Joey said. He stood on the dock looking down at Penelope, squinting in the sunshine. The Saturday morning ferry was approaching, its low horn sounding out on the ocean.

"Yes. Well, about seven weeks, give or take," Penelope said. She caressed his fingers in her hands and smiled.

"I'd tell you to be careful down here but I know you can handle yourself," Joey said. "You did a great job up on that roof."

"Thanks," Penelope said shyly. "I'm glad you were with me, though. I don't know what I would have done by myself."

"So Rose will probably go to jail for involuntary manslaughter because she was worried about a little competition from Emilio?"

"I guess, or she just couldn't handle all of the changes that are happening on the island," Penelope said. "I talked to Emilio and he said the charges against him have been dropped. He also said he's going to make Shane agree to have a portion of the restaurant's business be devoted to teaching. He wants to teach cooking classes for the local kids here, free of charge."

"Well, that's one good thing to come out of this mess," Joey said.

"I'm so relived Rebekkah woke up," Penelope said.

"Was she able to tell the police anything?" Joey asked.

"She confirmed the story that Emilio told, about them going to the house after the party, then leaving in a panic when they realized how far from home they were in a strange man's house. They got scared and ran."

Joey shook his head sadly. "Emilio might be a little reckless, but they were safer inside with him."

"She's still traumatized by the whole thing, mostly by losing her best friend. I hope that eventually she'll be okay. Arlena visited Rebekkah in the hospital, offered to help her start the drama club they had talked about on the set, if that's still something Rebekkah wants to do."

"Maybe that will be something good for her, when she's back on her feet at school," Joey offered.

They were quiet for a moment, thinking about everything that had happened and listening to the waves lapping against the dock.

"I'm going to miss you," Penelope said after a minute. She laid her head against his chest and listened to his heartbeat.

"Me too, Penny Blue," Joey said, gazing out at the water. "Listen, I know we're both busy and our schedules are crazy, but when you get home, I'd like to see you more often."

Penelope's heart fluttered in her chest, but she kept her expression neutral.

"Really?"

"Yeah," Joey said, a bit bashfully. "If you want to, and we both feel that way in a couple of months, I would like us to get more serious, take our relationship to the next level."

Waves started lapping against the dock as the ferry approached the slip, the captain slowing down to ease it up to the dock. Penelope saw a few expectant faces, happy beachgoers who were going to spend their Saturday experiencing some of Andrea Island's Old Florida charm.

"That sounds really nice, Joey," Penelope said, moving in to kiss him.

Joey kissed her back and then pulled away, looking into her eyes. "I don't want you to feel pressured or make any promises you don't want to keep. I just want to be with you."

Penelope smiled and kissed him again as the ferry passengers began to disembark onto the dock around them. "Joey, I want to be with you too," she said.

Joey's eyes flicked to the *Isn't She Lovely* in the furthest slip on the dock. He raised his arm and waved at Arlena and Max, who stood on the top deck watching them. They returned his wave and he said, "Because if you're interested in anyone else, I'm not looking for that kind of relationship. I want to be exclusive with the right person, and I feel like the right person for me is you."

Penelope looked at him, not sure how to respond. Finally she settled on, "Joey, I'm not interested in anyone else."

Joey smiled and shook his head. "Tell you what. You think about it for the rest of the time you're down here. And then we'll talk when you get back, see where we are."

Penelope nodded and said, "That sounds fair. I can't wait until this movie wraps and we can all get home."

"Are you tired of living in paradise, Penny Blue?"

"Paradise is much more than warm weather and sandy beaches. For me, it's being with the people you care about the most. You can be in paradise wherever you are if you have that."

The horn sounded behind them and Joey kissed Penelope again, then pulled away to gaze at her face.

"Okay, that's my cue," Joey said, picking up his suitcase and heading towards the ferry.

"Call me when you land, okay?" Penelope called to him. A warm aching sensation spread through her chest as he walked away.

Joey turned and waved. "Will do. I'll miss you."

"I'll miss you too," Penelope said, swallowing a lump in her throat.

The ferry pulled away from the dock and headed out to sea. Penelope watched it go for as long as she could still see it. When the ferry disappeared from sight, she turned and walked slowly down the dock to the *Isn't She Lovely*, smiling contently and waving lazily at the old fishermen as she passed by.

SHAWN REILLY SIMMONS

Shawn Reilly Simmons was born in Indiana, grew up in Florida, and began her professional career in New York City as a sales executive after graduating from the University of Maryland with a BA in English. Since then Shawn has worked as a bookstore manager, fiction editor, convention organizer, wine consultant and caterer. She has been on the Board of Directors of Malice Domestic since 2003, and is a founding member of The Dames of Detection. Cooking behind the scenes on movie sets perfectly combined two of her great loves, movies and food, and provides the inspiration for her series.

The Red Carpet Catering Mystery Series
By Shawn Reilly Simmons

MURDER ON A SILVER PLATTER (#1)
MURDER ON THE HALF SHELL (#2)
MURDER ON A DESIGNER DIET (#3)

Available at booksellers nationwide and online

Visit www.henerypress.com for details

Henery Press Mystery Books

And finally, before you go...
Here are a few other mysteries
you might enjoy:

FATAL BRUSHSTROKE

Sybil Johnson

An Aurora Anderson Mystery (#1)

A dead body in her garden and a homicide detective on her doorstep...

Computer programmer and tole-painting enthusiast Aurora (Rory) Anderson doesn't envision finding either when she steps outside to investigate the frenzied yipping coming from her own back yard. After all, she lives in Vista Beach, a quiet California beach community where violent crime is rare and murder even rarer.

Suspicion falls on Rory when the body buried in her flowerbed turns out to be someone she knows—her tole-painting teacher, Hester Bouquet. Just two weeks before, Rory attended one of Hester's weekend seminars, an unpleasant experience she vowed never to repeat. As evidence piles up against Rory, she embarks on a quest to identify the killer and clear her name. Can Rory unearth the truth before she encounters her own brush with death?

Available at booksellers nationwide and online

Visit www.henerypress.com for details

CROPPED TO DEATH

Christina Freeburn

A Faith Hunter Scrap This Mystery (#1)

Former US Army JAG specialist, Faith Hunter, returns to her West Virginia home to work in her grandmothers' scrapbooking store determined to lead an unassuming life after her adventure abroad turned disaster. But her quiet life unravels when her friend is charged with murder—and Faith inadvertently supplied the evidence. So Faith decides to cut through the scrap and piece together what really happened.

With a sexy prosecutor, a determined homicide detective, a handful of sticky suspects and a crop contest gone bad, Faith quickly realizes if she's not careful, she'll be the next one cropped.

Available at booksellers nationwide and online

Visit www.henerypress.com for details

FIT TO BE DEAD

Nancy G. West

An Aggie Mundeen Mystery (#1)

Aggie Mundeen, single and pushing forty, fears nothing but middle age. When she moves from Chicago to San Antonio, she decides she better shape up before anybody discovers she writes the column, "Stay Young with Aggie." She takes Aspects of Aging at University of the Holy Trinity and plunges into exercise at Fit and Firm.

Rusty at flirting and mechanically inept, she irritates a slew of male exercisers, then stumbles into murder. She'd like to impress the attractive detective with her sleuthing skills. But when the killer comes after her, the health club evacuates semi-clad patrons, and the detective has to stall his investigation to save Aggie's derriere.

Available at booksellers nationwide and online

Visit www.henerypress.com for details

DEATH WITH AN OCEAN VIEW

Noreen Wald

A Kate Kennedy Mystery (#1)

Nestled between fast track Ft. Lauderdale and nouveau riche Boca Raton, the once sleepy beach town of Palmetto is plagued by progress. The latest news has Ocean Vista condo board president Stella Sajak and other residents in an uproar. Developers plan to raze the property and put up a glitzy resort. But when Stella says she'll go to City Hall and fight this to the death, no one thinks to take her statement literally.

And when Kate begins to investigate the murder, she discovers that this little corner of the Sunshine State is cursed with corruption, unsavory characters, and a very dark cloud overhead.

Available at booksellers nationwide and online

Visit www.henerypress.com for details

A MUDDIED MURDER

Wendy Tyson

A Greenhouse Mystery (#1)

When Megan Sawyer gives up her big-city law career to care for her grandmother and run the family's organic farm and café, she expects to find peace and tranquility in her scenic hometown of Winsome, Pennsylvania. Instead, her goat goes missing, rain muddies her fields, the town denies her business permits, and her family's Colonial-era farm sucks up the remains of her savings.

Just when she thinks she's reached the bottom of the rain barrel, Megan and the town's hunky veterinarian discover the local zoning commissioner's battered body in her barn. Now Megan is thrust into the middle of a murder investigation—and she's the chief suspect. Can Megan dig through small-town secrets, local politics, and old grievances in time to find a killer before that killer strikes again?

Available at booksellers nationwide and online

Visit www.henerypress.com for details

Made in the USA
Lexington, KY
18 September 2017